## "You wanted me to kiss you," Jay said bluntly

Vicky couldn't deny it, but she had to protect herself somehow. "And because of that you think I—I'm easy game," she protested bitterly.

"Did I say so?" He moved his head, and she ached to press her lips against his throat. "Or is it because you kissed me back that you're getting so worked up? And you were, weren't you?"

She managed a small shrug. "It was only a kiss...."

"No, it damned well wasn't. You know it and I know it, too. Face up to it, Vicky. There's something between us that we both know. And I don't think of you as easy game," he added quietly.

She started to tremble as his lips touched hers again—and she knew she was lost....

**PENNY JORDAN** was constantly in trouble in school because of her inability to stop daydreaming—especially during French lessons. In her teens she was an avid romance reader, although it didn't occur to her to try writing one herself until she was older. "My first half-dozen attempts ended up ingloriously," she remembers, "but I persevered, and one manuscript was finished." She plucked up the courage to send it to a publisher, convinced her book would be rejected. It wasn't—and the rest is history! Penny is married and lives in Cheshire.

## Books by Penny Jordan

### HARLEQUIN PRESENTS
746—DARKER SIDE OF DESIRE
755—RULES OF THE GAME
761—CAMPAIGN FOR LOVING
770—WHAT YOU MADE ME
785—THE ONLY ONE
794—THE FRIENDSHIP BARRIER
809—THE SIX-MONTH MARRIAGE
818—TAKEN OVER
826—TIME FUSE
833—YOU OWE ME
850—EXORCISM
868—PERMISSION TO LOVE
883—INJURED INNOCENT

### HARLEQUIN SIGNATURE EDITION
LOVE'S CHOICES

These books may be available at your local bookseller.

Don't miss any of our special offers. Write to us at the following address for information on our newest releases.

Harlequin Reader Service
901 Fuhrmann Blvd., P.O. Box 1397, Buffalo, NY   14240
Canadian address: P.O. Box 2800, Postal Station A,
5170 Yonge St., Willowdale, Ont.   M2N 6J3

# PENNY JORDAN

# the hard man

## Harlequin Books

TORONTO • NEW YORK • LONDON
AMSTERDAM • PARIS • SYDNEY • HAMBURG
STOCKHOLM • ATHENS • TOKYO • MILAN

Harlequin Presents first edition July 1986
ISBN 0-373-10897-4

Original hardcover edition published in 1985
by Mills & Boon Limited

# CHAPTER ONE

'EVERYTHING seems to be in order.'

Watching the dark head of his latest client bend over the document he was signing, Philip Sterne reflected that it was rare indeed in his long legal experience to meet an entrepeneur who managed to combine decisiveness with intelligence in such equal measures. But then that was no doubt the secret of Jay Brentford's meteoric rise into the higher echelons of business success.

From the time he had taken over his first company less than ten years ago, he had seldom been out of the financial press. This latest acquisition—the purchase of a small, rather run-down construction company based in a sleepy Cotswold village—might seem rather out of keeping at first sight, but Philip prided himself on his own business acumen, and could quite easily see why a man with the resources that Jay Brentford had at his command could want to add a small, old-established but failing local firm to his assets, especially if he was hoping to tender for the proposed new motorway that was going to be built locally.

Philip watched as he signed his name, quickly, and efficiently with no evidence of any flourish. A hard man, or so he had read, and he certainly looked the part; the tall, lean body cloaked in its formal dark business suit held more than a faint suggestion of whiplash strength, and Philip guessed that the cool grey eyes could chill with demoralising speed if their owner ever happened to be faced with something or someone who did not match his exacting standards. How old was he? Mid-to late thirties?

The sound of his new client's voice, faintly harsh and abrasive dragged him out of his mental reverie.

'Somewhere to stay?'

'Yes, a good hotel. I shall need a room for a couple of weeks. There are still some business ends I want to tie up.'

Philip frowned. 'I'm afraid Little Camwater has only one hotel—The Bells—and I know it's fully booked up,' he told him regretfully. 'Your best bet would probably be Gloucester, or failing that, perhaps one of the tourist hotels in one of the other villages.'

'Tourist hotels?' Jay shook his head, frowning slightly. The sort of hotel the solicitor was describing would no doubt be full of just the sort of people he didn't want to meet right now.

Taking over Camwater Construction had been an impulse decision, and one which the remainder of his main board still did not entirely approve of, even though in the end reluctantly they had backed him. They could not see why they could not tender for the motorway contract without taking over another company specifically to do so. After all, their existing companies had all the facilities they would need, and if their tender were to be successful they would need all the capital they had just to ensure their line of supplies. However, Jay had overruled them, pointing out that the government both at London and local level would look more favourably on a tender with local connections, with at least some interest in the area in which they were to work. His mouth compressed as he dwelt on the problems ahead of him if they were successful in their tender. The construction of new motorways was always something that aroused intense local feeling. This particular one had been carefully planned so as not to despoil the beautiful countryside through which it would run. Nevertheless, there had already been considerable opposition.

Pushing aside the sensation of bleak tiredness seeping into his bones, he dragged his thoughts away from the problems ahead of him and instead tried to concentrate on the more immediate one of finding somewhere to stay. If he couldn't find a hotel he would have to use the house—something he had no particular desire to do, because then he would need to find staff. Grimacing faintly, he wondered if Laine had not after all been right, and if he should not have taken a break after that last gruelling contract in the Middle East before driving down here.

Laine ... His mouth curled faintly. He knew quite well what she was angling for, but marriage wasn't among his plans for the future. Not now— perhaps not ever—and certainly not to a woman like Laine, who he knew quite well had other lovers beside himself. 'No hotel. Damn!' He was only aware of having spoken out loud when he heard Philip murmuring, half-apologetically, 'Well there is somewhere—not an hotel—but an excellent boarding house, run by another of my clients as it happens.' Philip saw the dark, raised eyebrows, and despite his fifty-odd years flushed beneath the implied cynicism of it.

'Touting for business for them? Is that part of your service?'

'Not at all.'

Noting the stiff disapproval in the solicitor's voice Jay wished the sarcastic words unsaid. The trouble was he was far too much on edge and had been for weeks. That Middle Eastern contract, while highly remunerative, had been a real s.o.b. Everything that could have gone wrong had done so, and in the end he had had to spend eight weeks out there which he had not been able to spare, just to ensure that the contract was completed without invoking any of the penalty clauses. Dealing with his principals had involved walking on eggshells, something he wasn't used to doing, and it had left him on edge and exhausted. He apologised briefly, watching the relief seep up under Philip's embarrassed reserve.

'A boarding house, you say?' He grimaced faintly, 'Well, if there's nothing better.'

He was visualising the type of boarding house he well remembered from his teens; the days when he himself had worked in the construction industry, as a labourer. God, those had been hard times, but the money had been good and he had managed to save enough to start up his own small business. Enough to offer Jenny marriage. He had also been young and foolish enough to believe that she loved him as much as he loved her. He had soon learned better. Even now he could remember, in exact detail, the night she had told him that their engagement was off; that she was going to marry her father's business partner. She had avoided his eyes as she handed him back his ring, and even now he could still taste the bitterness of gall and helpless, hopeless pain as it rose up in his throat.

Oh, he had argued with her, pleaded with her

not to go through with it, pointing out that James Oliver was twenty years her senior, but she had made up her mind. She could not envisage for herself the sort of life she would have as his wife, following him from construction site to site, often living in a beat-up old caravan, while he ploughed every bit of profit he made back into his struggling business. To her, he saw then, the dream, which seemed so bright and gleaming to him, was no more than a tinsel image, and one she shrank from, preferring the security and order of her father's already established world.

In the end he had had to leave her. Then twenty-four, he had thought she had broken his heart, but now he knew better. Hearts did not break, they merely hardened.

'If you like I can ring up and see if Vicky has a vacancy?' Philip was saying. 'She should do at this time of the year. Things are normally quite quiet. Camwater isn't on the main tourist track, and it's usually high summer before Vicky gets fully booked up. People come year after year to stay with her, once they've discovered her,' he continued, a rare smile illuminating his face. 'It's marvellous, how she's managed to keep that place going. When Henry died I advised her to sell it, but she wouldn't. She insisted that she had to keep it for Charles—her stepson,' he explained to Jay, shaking his head slightly. 'I never thought she'd manage it. The Old Vicarage is a lovely building, no doubt about that, but to maintain and run it—and to bring up Charles and the twins ...' He broke off as though sensing his client's boredom with the subject, and reached for his telephone.

'Get me Mrs Moreton at the Old Vicarage will you please, Madge?' he asked his secretary.

Whilst he was waiting, Jay strode over to the window and stood looking out of it down into the small square below. Philip Sterne's offices were on the second floor of a small row of late Georgian terraced houses. Opposite from them was a tangle of Tudor buildings, and the square itself still retained its ancient cobbles. Today was market day but Jay stared down at the mêlée of people surging round the wooden stalls without really seeing them. He himself had been brought up in the North, in a small cotton mill town that ran like a narrow ribbon in the valley between brooding Pennine hills. When he was eighteen he had discovered that the parents who had brought him up were in reality his aunt and uncle, and that his mother had been his aunt's younger sister, who had 'got herself into trouble' in Manchester with a seaman who had left the area long before his mother had known she was carrying his child.

No one had ever been actively unkind to him, but somehow the discovery that he was not really the son of his foster parents had enabled him to tear himself free of the valley, which had always in some undefinable way stifled him. He had hated not being able to see over the hills ... the sensation of being closed in ... shut off from the mainstream of life. His aunt and uncle had not been entirely sorry to see him go. He had been a responsibility they had willingly shouldered, perceiving it their duty to do so, but he had never truly been one of them. There had always been an element of the cuckoo in the nest about him. For instance, he had been the only one in the family to get a pass to the local grammar school, and his obvious intelligence had always somehow set him apart from his brother and sisters. He still kept in touch with them, but they like him preferred a distant relationship to a closer one. They found it easier to deal with his success when they viewed him as a cousin ... somehow apart from the family instead of being part of it. He was godfather to his eldest cousin's son and religiously remembered to send a gift of money to the boy every birthday and Christmas.

'Vicky?' He heard Philip Sterne laugh and reflected cynically that the as yet unseen Vicky obviously knew quite well how to get round the old boy, if the amused sound of his laughter was anything to go by.

'Do you have an empty room at the moment? You do? Excellent. I have a client in need of somewhere to stay for a fortnight.' There was a brief pause, and then Jay heard Philip saying in a pleased tone. 'Yes, I think he'd appreciate that. I'll give him directions to you ... Yes, very well, thank-you, and how are all of you?' More laughter before the receiver was replaced, and Jay wasn't aware that he was frowning until he heard Philip saying rather mildly. 'Vicky is my goddaughter, Mr Brentford.' He smiled briefly and then added in a more formal tone. 'She does have a room free, and in fact suggested that, since you might like to have your own sitting room as well, she would give you the small self-contained suite that Henry had made for his late mother. That way you will have a certain amount of privacy in which to conduct your work, although of course, Vicky will provide all your meals.'

That way also no doubt 'Vicky' could charge him a good deal more than she would for a mere single room, was Jay's cynical thought, but he allowed nothing of his feeling to show in his expression, guessing that if he did so, Philip Sterne would immediately leap to the defence of his precious goddaughter.

'How far from Camwater is this place?' he asked instead, aware of a certain brusqueness in his voice, but unable to do anything about it.

'Oh, less than five miles.'

He listened as Philip gave him directions and then glanced briefly at his watch. Just gone three o'clock. Too late to bother about lunch. He might as well go direct to this Old Vicarage place and dump his case. He would have to ring London and confirm that he had signed the contract, and he would also have to ring Laine.

It was half-past three before he manoeuvred the long bonnet of his steel-grey BMW out of the narrow confines of the small market town heading in the direction Philip Sterne had instructed him to take.

The early December afternoon was already turning to dusk, a faint haw of frost whitening the hedgerows. Jay noticed it without much pleasure, reflecting on what a hard winter would do to his contract schedules, especially those relating to work they were doing in the North of Scotland for one of the larger oil companies. The road forked and he slowed down slightly even though he had the right of way, cursing as almost out of nowhere a boy on a bicycle shot out of the side road right in front of his car. The fact that he chose to swerve rather than brake was an instinctive judgment made by the same inner consciousness which had already noticed the drop in temperature and the frosting hedgerows. One of them loomed up ahead of him now, etched sharply in black and white, wicked thorns, scraping hideously against the front

fender of his car. He felt the lurch as the front wheel
hit the ditch and wrenched hard on the wheel,
fighting to keep the car on the road and bring it to
a standstill.

'I say, I'm most dreadfully sorry . . .'

The sudden intrusion of the youthful male voice
into the thick silence of the car brought him out
of his stunned realisation of how narrowly he had
avoided mowing down the cyclist, and with the
realisation came a fierce reactionary wave of
anger.

He turned to the passenger door and leaned
across to the partially open window, his eyes the
biting cold of the arctic seas that Philip Sterne had
so accurately visualised they could be as he gritted,
'Just what the hell do you think you were doing?
Did no one ever teach you any road sense? Don't
you *know* what a giveway sign means, damn you?'

Hazel eyes held the bleak anger of his own with
steady regard, a faint tinge of colour suddenly
driven out of the boyish face as it turned
ominously pale. Cursing, Jay thrust open his door
and strode round to the passenger side. The boy
had dismounted from his bike and was leaning
over it, straight tow-coloured hair hiding his
expression.

'Take it easy. Come on . . .' Jay opened the
passenger door and half pushed the boy into it.
Tall and thin he looked about fourteen. He was
wearing school uniform and Jay guessed he was on
his way home. His bike was well maintained and
illuminated, old but well looked after, and as he
ran idle fingers over the paintwork Jay was
suddenly transported backwards in time. God,
how he remembered his own first proper bike. It
had been his pride and joy. He too, had used it for

school. He grimaced faintly, remembering the
forbidden joy of riding it behind a heavy lorry,
using the tail draught. The anger drained out of
him, to be replaced by a weary lethargy.

Stooping he picked up the bike and strode
round to the back of the car.

His actions alerted the boy and he struggled to
get out of the car, his face ashen with shock and
reaction. 'Hey . . .' his voice was husky, probably
just on the point of breaking into manhood, Jay
guessed.

'It's okay,' he responded laconically. 'I'm not
about to throw it into the ditch and you after it,
although it would be no more than you deserve.
Hasn't your father ever warned you not to race
out at a junction like that without stopping to
look?'

'My father's dead.'

He said it reluctantly, and Jay quashed the brief
feeling of guilt that stabbed at him.

'Your mother then,' he amended curtly, 'or
whoever the hell is in charge of you. Where do you
live, I'll give you a lift back there?'

'There's no need, I can walk.' Once again the
boy was making to get out of the car and Jay
swore abruptly, suddenly realising how weary and
tired he was himself. 'Don't be so damned stupid,'
he demanded angrily. 'You're far too shocked to
be walking anywhere, and besides, I wouldn't trust
you not to get back on that damned bike and
attempt to give some other unfortunate driver a
heart attack.'

In the thin light he saw a reluctant grin touch
the boy's mouth and his muscles relaxed slightly.
What could have been a fatal accident had been
averted: the shock of what had happened had no

doubt taught the boy a lesson he would long remember if his white face was anything to go by, and he was too tired himself to spend any further time lecturing him; he would leave that task to the boy's mother.

'Where do you live?' he asked, fitting the bike into the BMW's roomy boot and closing the lid. 'I'm making for a place called the Old Vicarage.'

The quality of the boy's silence made his eyes narrow in a thoughtful study of the youthful face as he got back into the car. 'Come on,' he demanded curtly, 'tell me where you live.'

'At the Old Vicarage.' The admission came reluctantly and Jay grimaced slightly as he tried to recall what Philip Sterne had told him about his prospective landlady.

'So you must be Mrs Moreton's . . .'

'Stepson,' he was informed briefly. He watched as the boy bit his lower lip, a wealth of emotions struggling for supremacy. 'You're still going to stay with us aren't you?' he asked at length, surprising Jay a little by the nature of his request. He had expected the boy to ask him not to say anything to his stepmother about the accident.

'Ma needs the money,' his passenger explained frankly, when he didn't reply. 'We don't get many boarders during the winter, and it's hard for her to make ends meet. Mr Sterne thinks she should sell the house, but she won't 'cos it's been in my family for ever, practically, and she thinks I should have it. I've told her I'm not bothered about it,' he added, 'but she won't listen to me. You will still stay, won't you?' He went quiet for a minute and then added, rather gruffly. 'Ma doesn't like me using my bike in the winter, but I need it for my paper round. I could pay for any damage to your

car out of my wages ... it might take several
weeks ...'

To judge from the damage the thorn hedge was
likely to have done to his paintwork Jay guessed
that repayment would be more likely to be a
matter of months, if not years, rather than weeks,
but he said nothing, curiously drawn to the boy
now that his initial anger had faded.

'Mr Philip Sterne informed me that I'd be lucky
to find myself any alternative accommodation
locally at this time of year, so you're fairly safe on
that score.'

A look of relief crossed the boy's face, and he
said easily, 'Well all the big hotels will be booked
up for Christmas now.'

Christmas. Jay had forgotten how close it was.
The last hectic weeks in the Middle East had
driven all thoughts of Christmas and its celebration
right out of his mind.

'Turn left here,' his passenger directed, suddenly
relaxing a little ... 'It isn't far now.'

As she filled the trough with steaming mash for
the hens, Vicky wondered if it was true that one
always favoured the time of the year when one was
born above all other seasons. Certainly the fact
that she had been born towards the end of
November almost ensured that she was a child of
winter, but could that alone explain what to others
was her totally inexplicable love of such a bleak
time of year? Snow had been forecast that
morning, but as she contemplated the clear sky
and freezing drop in temperature she reflected that
it would probably be a couple of days before it
reached them. She had lived nearly all her life in
the Cotswolds, apart from a brief spell at Bristol
when she had been at university.

Sighing faintly she turned away from the hens and walked back to the house, the kitchen door stood open and through it she could hear the twins quarrelling—loudly.

'Stop it you two,' she called out as she put the hens' bucket down and tugged off her wellingtons before going in.

The dark red quarry tiled floor shone from the polishing she had given it earlier in the afternoon, and she grimaced faintly knowing from experience that it wouldn't stay clean long. The Old Vicarage was a beautiful house, but it wore her out keeping it clean. Her friends told her that she ought to invest in more labour-saving floor coverings than the rich parquet and quarry tiles that demanded so much time and attention but there simply wasn't the money to spare, even if she had wanted to do so.

'What's going on?' she demanded of the squabbling pair of dark-haired children seated at the wooden table, adding severely, 'You're supposed to be doing your homework.'

'Jamie pinched my ruler,' the smaller of the two piped up, lifting mock-tragic, dark grey eyes to meet her own.

'It's not your ruler Julie, it's mine,' her brother claimed hotly, rudely shoving her with his elbow, eyes as dark and appealing as his sister's, fixing on his mother's face.

Sighing faintly, Vicky reflected that the mother of twins such as her pair needed the wisdom of Solomon and the patience of Job, not to mention a host of other attributes, including a spare pair of eyes, preferably in the back of one's head.

'It *is* my ruler,' Julie interrupted, refusing to let the squabble die. 'Look it's got a J scratched in this corner.'

She presented the ruler for Vicky's scrutiny. 'Yes and it's my J,' Jamie argued hotly. 'It's my ruler Ma . . .'

It had been a long and difficult day with a 'phone call from the bank manager commenting on the meagre funds in her account, and a large bill from the gas board, and listening to them Vicky felt the last of her dearly held patience slipping away. 'How many times have I told you not to call me "Ma",' she demanded wrathfully of her son.

'But Charles calls you "Ma".'

'Because she isn't really his mother,' Julie told her brother scornfully, 'Ma is only Charles' stepmother . . .'

'That's enough from the pair of you,' Vicky announced feeling thoroughly exasperated, and wondering what it was about her terrible twosome that sometimes made her feel as though she had totally lost control of any given situation which involved them.

'Hyperactive,' Doctor Robinson had designated them when at two years old they had more than fully proved the correctness of the phrase the 'terrible twos'. 'Intelligent and lively,' was how their first teacher had described them when they first started school. Perishing brats was Charles' lordly, elder brotherly favourite description and love them though she did, there were times when Vicky felt as though they had pushed her to the end of her tether.

'Get on with your homework both of you,' she commanded briskly. 'We've got a new lodger arriving tonight, so supper will be a bit later than usual.'

'A new lodger . . . goody! Does that mean I can have a new bike for Christmas after all?' demanded the irrepressible Jamie. At nine years old he was well aware of the connection between their lodgers and their income. Sighing faintly Vicky shook her head. She hated having to disappoint them, especially at Christmas time. On the whole they were good kids, who didn't ask for much in the way of material things. It had been a struggle to keep the vicarage on after Henry's death. Both of them had known he was ill and that he would die, but neither of them had expected his death to come so suddenly . . . also surely Henry had not realised the risk he was taking in investing his money in those Australian shares.

Sighing faintly, Vicky pushed her hair out of her eyes. It was pointless going over the past, what was done was done, and she was determined to do all she could to keep the Old Vicarage. Friends thought she was mad and told her so, but then they would not understand the sense of loyalty that made her so determined to preserve Charles' inheritance. None of them really understood her relationship with her stepson . . . but then none of them understood either, the sense of debt and gratitude she felt towards Henry . . . if it hadn't been for him, both she and the twins would have simply been three more statistics; she would have simply been another unmarried mother with two illegitimate children to bring up, a girl with half a university education and no degree. How on earth would she have got a job? How on earth would she have been able to support herself and the twins, if Henry hadn't offered her the security of marriage?

They had talked about it of course . . . he had been a friend of Vicky's grandmother's before the latter's death, and when she had found herself 'in trouble' as the description went, he had been the

one to coax her into telling him the truth. He had
been a widower then for almost five years—his
wife had died giving birth to Charles. He had not
married until he was forty, and Sheila had been
the same age; too old, perhaps, for a first child.
Their marriage would be one of convenience only,
he had told her carefully, without any physical
union. Vicky had been glad of that, shrinking from
the thought of repeating with anyone the shaming
experience which had resulted in the conception of
the twins, but shame of course had come later,
when she had realised what she had done: when—
why not be honest with herself?—when she had
sobered up enough to allow the anguish filled
snatches of memory to surface past her mammoth
hangover.

At first she had demurred. How could she allow
him to marry her and shoulder her burdens, but
then he had told her that the arrangement would
not be entirely one-sided. He was dying he told
her, of a wasting disease that would progressively
worsen. He would die before Charles reached
adulthood and then what would become of his
son? Neither he nor Sheila had any relatives, nor
any friends close enough to entrust with the
guardianship of his only child. Once she realised
that she would be giving something to their
relationship and not just taking from it Vicky had
changed her mind. He had given her time to decide
properly, pointing out to her that marriage to him
would preclude her from any romantic involve-
ments with boys of her own age but she had
simply shuddered and told him that she wanted
none. At eighteen she was convinced she knew all
she wanted to know about the male sex. In the
event he had not lived as long as he had hoped,

dying when the twins were six months old and Charles just five, and since then she had struggled to keep the family and their home together, mainly by taking in summer lodgers.

A stay of at least two weeks. Mentally she added up figures, and allowed herself to feel a mild amount of relief. That should be enough to cover the gas bill at least, and hopefully would leave something towards next year's rates. Thank God Charles had been clever enough to get that scholarship, without it ... She had been both pleased and proud when Charles won a coveted scholarship to his father's old school, and had scrimped and scraped to buy him his first brand new uniform, not wanting him to suffer the indignity of going to his new school in someone else's hand me downs. She would do far better to count her blessings rather than mope about what could not be, she told herself as both dark curly heads dutifully bent over school books. A nuisance though they sometimes were, at least the twins were healthy and clever, if their teachers were to be believed. In addition to that they got on well with Charles and he with them. As soon as they had been old enough to understand she had explained to them that Henry had not been their father. So far they had asked very few questions about their missing parent's identity, but already she was dreading the day when they did. What on earth could she say to them? The truth? That she simply did not know? That their father was a man she had met at a party when she had been too drunk to refuse his advances and that she had been as dismayed as she was disbelieving when she woke up to find herself in a strange bedroom with him.

But not half as stricken as she had been to

discover that she was pregnant, she thought grimly. She simply hadn't known where to turn. Advice hadn't been as freely available then as it was now. In the end she had gone home to her grandmother, only to find her seriously ill in hospital suffering from the effects of a bad fall. Henry had been on his way to break the news to her, and it had been then that she had broken down and confessed the truth. Dear Henry. He had been more like a father to her than a husband. In fact in many ways he had been the father she had never had; the father that the twins now needed so desperately she reflected grimly, recalling to mind several of their more dare-devil exploits. While they worked at one end of the table she busied herself at the other.

Philip's 'phone call had been something of a surprise, and she had been forced to raid the freezer to find something a little more appetising for their guest than the plain fare they would normally have had. In reality they were luckier than most she reflected; the vicarage had a large kitchen garden, which even though it meant a good deal of back-breaking work, did provide them with a year-round supply of fresh vegetables, in addition there was the orchard where the hens ran and provided them with free-range eggs. She also had a business arrangement with a local farmer's wife to whom she supplied bottled preserved fruit in exchange for butter and milk and sometimes even a side of bacon. On the whole they did not do too badly, certainly the children were well fed, even if sometimes she herself wished there was more money to spare for essentials such as bills and clothes.

'What are you making?'

Julie raised her dark curly head from her books to study her mother.

In appearance the twins were as alike as two peas in a pod, but neither of them resembled her. No . . . it must be their father they took after; that shadowy figure she remembered as nothing more than hard hands in the darkness of the night, and a dark sleek head on the pillow in the cold bitter light of dawn. He had been older than she was, with a man's body, whilst hers had still been that of a girl, his features rough-hewn, and hard even in sleep.

A quiver of something shivered through her stomach, and she tried to blot out the memory and the aching wave of self-disgust that always followed it. Him she could understand at least in part . . . what man would resist a girl who had made herself so easy to pick up and seduce? But what manner of man could he be, this unknown father of her children, not to have realised that she had been little more than a child herself? What manner of man was he to take to his bed a girl so plainly drunk and unaware of what she was doing or who she was with that she had lost her virginity before she had even realised what was happening? And he had not been gentle with her. Her body had born the bruises to prove that. She had ached with pain for days afterwards, and even now she could vividly recall the stunned sense of disbelief with which she had gathered up her scattered clothes and slunk from his room, so early that even the hotel staff were not up and about.

At first she had been too relieved to discover that none of her university friends had realised what had happened, to dwell on any possible repercussions from her behaviour. She had gone to the party in the first place with a group of them, innocently drinking the 'fruit punch' she had been given, without even realising what was in it ... until it was far too late. She had some hazy recollections of dancing with the man ... of giggling when he held her close to his body ... of him saying something about her leaving with him ... and even of making no protest when he dragged her away from her friends and outside into the thick dark. What on earth he had been doing at the party in the first place she had had no idea. It had been held by the older brother of another graduate, at the home of their parents, who apparently had been away.

She could vaguely remember the man arriving and looking formal and out of place in his dark business suit. He had been drinking, too, she could remember, smelling it on his breath. He had asked for someone called 'Jenny' she could remember that. Jenny was apparently their host's cousin, or so she had discovered later, but after that ... after she had left the house with him everything was a blur, until that sharp intimate pain that had rent aside her intoxicated veils of ignorance ... and then much, much later, the shame of waking up in the morning and discovering herself in bed with a stranger, her body violated and torn from his possession of her.

# CHAPTER TWO

'MA, I can hear a car.' Jamie threw down his pen and got down from the table, heading for the door.

'I'll see to it, Jamie,' Vicky told him repressively. 'You get on with your homework.' She had been so deeply engrossed in her own thoughts that she hadn't heard the car, but she could do so now. As she walked briskly into the hall she gave a quick glance at the clock. Where on earth was Charles? He should have have been home half an hour ago. She suppressed a brief sigh. It worried her to know that he was riding home alone on these dark winter nights, but she also knew that he hated her to fuss. It seemed unbelievable how fast he was growing up; he was fourteen already, his voice breaking. Tugging off her apron she deposited it on the hall table. Philip had said nothing more about their new lodger other than that he was a businessman who needed a base for at least a couple of weeks. In three weeks time it would be Christmas. Repressing another faint sigh she tried to stem the guilt she felt at knowing how unlikely James was to get the BMX he was so desperate for. It was at times like these, when she had to deny the children the material possessions which most of their friends possessed, that she felt most guilty. It did no good reminding herself that they were well fed and warm; that they were loved and that they had freedom and space around them. She opened the door and stood beneath the porch light, its glare falling directly on her face, revealing it in minute detail to the man standing just outside the shadow of the porch.

She was nothing like what Jay had expected. For a start she was tiny, barely more than five foot two or three, and so slim that her fragility half shocked him. He had been expecting a buxom countrywoman with red cheeks and untidy hair, comfortably plump and somehow motherly. This woman was none of these things. For a start she looked far too young. Her hair, a deep, glorious auburn was caught back off her face with a green ribbon that echoed the colour of her eyes, but several strands had escaped to curl wildly round her face. It was an unusual face, Jay decided, studying her covertly; delicately boned and as fragile as the rest of her, and yet there was something about it . . . something in her expression that hinted at a strength that both intrigued and moved him. Lost in a contemplative study of his own unusual reaction to her—it had been a long, long time since he had looked at any woman so intently—he had forgotten his young passenger.

Vicky, just on the point of extending her hand to greet her unexpected guest, saw him turn, her body tensing with surprise as she watched Charles clambering out of the large car parked just alongside the door.

'Charles!'

As her anxious glance slid from Charles to the car and then back again her stepson said uncertainly, 'Don't fuss, Ma. I'm okay . . .'

'Okay? Alarm bells went off in Vicky's brain. 'Charles . . .' she began ominously hurrying towards him.

A hand on her shoulder stopped her. She tensed

beneath it, realising as she did so how long it was since a man had touched her, even as impersonally as this. After Henry's death she had shunned male company, too distraught by his death, and the responsibilities it had brought her, to do more than will herself to live from one day to the next. Since then there had been men of course, who she sensed were interested in her, but she had always retreated from them. What single man would want or afford to take on her and her responsibilities? And there was no room in her life for a purely sexual liaison. There were times when she looked enviously at those of her women friends who seemed happily married, but she was sensible enough to know that what she envied was the fact that they had someone to share life's trials and tribulations. What had happened to her as a student had taught her to be cautious with the male sex. The man who had fathered the twins wasn't entirely to blame; she was honest enough to admit that. She had gone with him willingly enough, but surely he must have realised how young and inexperienced she was ... She remembered how she had noted that he was older than anyone else at the party, although there was not much else she could remember about him, just an impression of dark hair, as vigorously masculine and strong as his body ... a sensation of not really being there for him as an individual that had left her feeling tainted when she remembered it in the days that followed, but nothing more.

'Charles,' she exclaimed worried again, 'What . . .?'

'A slight accident—nothing to worry about.' The male voice was cool and yet reassuring, the fingers still curling round her upper arm, imparting a warmth and reassurance that left her almost dizzy.

'It was my fault, Ma.' Charles' voice rose to a squeak and then deepened. 'I wasn't looking where I was going . . . I rode out in front of him . . .'

Jay could feel the sudden increase of tension, even before he saw the accusation in the green eyes that suddenly met his own. Her face was frost white, and for a moment he thought she might actually faint, but then the anger died from her eyes, and shaking slightly Vicky pulled out of his grasp, and said to her stepson. 'Charles, how many times have I warned you about riding that bike?' She turned to Jay anxiety still darkening her eyes. 'If there's any damage to your car . . .'

As she said the words, Vicky was glancing at the obviously expensive vehicle parked on her drive, wondering bleakly where on earth she was going to get the money to pay for any damage that might have been done, but to her relief the man watching her simply shook his head and said calmly. 'Nothing I'm not covered for. I'd better introduce myself,' he added. 'I'm Jay Brentford, I believe Philip Sterne . . .'

'Yes. Yes . . . Mr Brentford, Philip did tell me to expect you,' Vicky interrupted. Although she smiled at him, Jay was aware of a certain reserve in her, and put it down to her anxiety about the boy, who was still lingering by the steps.

'I'll give you a hand with your bike,' he offered, turning back to him, but Charles shook his head. 'No . . . no thank-you, Sir, I can manage it okay. I'll lock up the hens while I'm out, Ma,' he called over his shoulder to Vicky as he headed back to the car.

Not a very good note to arrive on Jay reflected

wryly as he followed Victoria inside the house, and then up a long flight of stairs.

'Philip said that you had work to do, so I've put you in what is virtually a self-contained suite,' she informed him, pausing on the landing. 'If you wish to have your meals alone there, then that is fine.'

As he heard her speaking, Jay was surprised by his depth of pleasure in the faint huskiness of her voice. Snap out of it, he jeered at himself. You're letting yourself be seduced by the happy family myth. She paused on the dimly lit landing and opened a door, stepping inside. Jay followed her. He was in a pleasant, if somewhat shabby, sitting room. Under the large window was a desk, equipped with its own light and a telephone. The room also housed a comfortable looking sofa, a couple of chairs and a table. The crackle of logs from the fireplace startled him a little at first. It had been years since he had been in a room that boasted an open fire.

'The bedroom is to the right,' Vicky told him, 'and the bathroom through it on the left. We normally have supper at five-thirty in the evening, but of course if you want a later evening meal . . .'

She wanted him to eat alone, Jay recognised and for some perverse reason heard himself saying blandly, 'No, I don't want to put you to any trouble. I'll eat with you, if that's okay?'

He could sense her discomfort and felt momentarily ashamed of himself. He had barely met the woman and yet for some reason he was reacting to her in a way he couldn't remember reacting to any woman in a long time—if ever.

'That will be fine, Mr Brentford.' Vicky deliberately tried to keep her voice cool and level, and yet she sensed that he knew he had disturbed her. What on earth was wrong with her? Many of their guests preferred to share their meals with them, and in fact it made life easier for her if they did, and yet for some reason this man made her feel as uneasy as a cat in the presence of a large dog.

'Jay, please . . .'

It was more of a command than a request and stubbornly Vicky fought against it, not wanting to allow him to breach the barrier of formality she had erected between them, but knowing that to refuse to use his forename now would seem both childish and suspect, and knowing also that in accepting his permission to use his first name she had given him tacit authority to use her own.

'I'll leave you to unpack . . . Supper will be ready in an hour.'

As she made her way back downstairs, she tried to rationalise why this new lodger should make her feel so uncomfortable and prickly. Was it perhaps because it was the first time they had had only one boarder—and a man on his own at that? Usually their lodgers were older, retired couples, or young families.

Snap out of it, she advised herself as she walked back into the kitchen.

Charles had come in, and was washing his hands under the tap. He looked so thin and gangly standing there, she thought, the tense set of his shoulders informing her that he was already anticipating her lecture.

It was true that she had warned him often about the dangers of riding his bike, but on this occasion she sensed that the shock of the accident would accomplish far more than any lecture from her, so instead she walked across to him, giving him a brief hug and she said lightly, 'Thanks for locking up the hens.'

'It's okay.' His voice was gruff. 'He seems all right, doesn't he? The new lodger, I mean?'

'Mm ...' Vicky kept her voice deliberately neutral.

'He's got a super car. A BMW.'

She was a little surprised at the fervour in Charles' voice. Normally he didn't pay much attention to their guests. He worried about the vicarage and its upkeep, just as she did, but she tried to shield him as much as she could from their financial problems. He was too young to be burdened by them yet. It wasn't his fault that Henry had died almost penniless. She knew that initially when she came back to the village there had been speculation about Henry and herself. She even suspected there were those who suspected she had married him for his money, which wasn't strictly true. She and Henry had struck a bargain to benefit them both.

There had been those after Henry died, and they included Philip, who had advised her to sell the house and buy something smaller, investing the excess to provide her with an income, but she considered that the house was a sacred trust she had to pass on to Charles.

'Finished.' She looked up as Julie closed her exercise book. 'Me, too,' Jamie echoed. 'Can we go and watch TV now, Ma?'

'Only until supper's ready,' she told them. As she watched them go, she felt a faint twinge of misgiving. So far the twins had accepted the fact that they had no father. She had explained very simply to them when they were small that Henry was not their father, and they had accepted this in

the way that small children do. After all, they were
not the only children at school to come from a
one-parent family, and any gossip which there
might have been at the time of her return to the
village had died long ago. But one day soon they
were going to ask her more questions. It was only
natural that they should want to know more about
their father. But what could she tell them? That
they were the result of a particularly unloving one-
night stand? Another twinge of guilt struck her.
How could she burden them with the knowledge
of what their father was? How could she taint their
lives with her own brief and bitter memories of
him? It was a problem that was weighing more and
more heavily on her heart as time went past, but
she could see no real answer to it, unless she was
to lie to them. Even then what could she say that
would both satisfy their curiosity and prevent
them from wanting to discover more? She had no
idea of their father's identity it was true, but had
she wanted to might she not have been able to
discover more? It would have been a simple
enough task to make enquiries of her friends at
university. But she had not wanted to know
more—far from it.

At five-thirty on the dot Jay came downstairs.
Vicky saw him as she hurried through the hall in
the direction of the dining room.

He had changed, and showered too, she noticed,
taking in the still half dampness of his hair. The
formal business suit and crisp white shirt were
gone and in their place he was wearing cords and a
checked shirt. The cords hugged the long, lean
lines of his legs, and as Vicky felt her glance drawn
helplessly along the length of him, she was aware
of certain disturbing sensations prickling warningly

inside herself. It was so unlike her to be aware of any man that it was several seconds before she realised what they were. When, hot-cheeked with embarrassment she managed to drag her gaze away, it was with the uncomfortable knowledge that he was every bit as aware of her reaction to him as she had been herself. It was true there had been nothing in his polite inscrutability to tell her this, but she knew it all the same. What on earth was the matter with her? Was she suddenly at twenty-seven developing the pangs of a sexually frustrated widow? Why? They were not something she had ever experienced before. She and Henry had not lived sexually as man and wife in any case, and before him her only sexual experience had been with the twins' father . . . Shuddering slightly as much in shock as her own overwhelming reaction to him as anything else, Vicky stepped through the door that Jay held open for her, unaware as she did so that he was studying her every bit as intently as she had done him.

That sudden leap of sexual awareness between them had been something Jay would have had to have been blind not to see. He had experienced it before—or at least he had been on the receiving end of it before, he reflected cynically. A man did not make it to his age and status in life without being on the receiving end of a fair amount of feminine advances, but since Jenny's defection he had been coolly clinical in all his dealings with the female sex, sleeping with them, enjoying them sexually, but not allowing himself to become emotionally involved, and yet here he was reacting like an overgrown schoolboy to a woman he had only just met. Her nervously defensive manner towards him puzzled him slightly. It was more the sort of thing he would have expected from a shy teenager rather than a grown woman— a widow with three children in her care as well. He remembered that Philip had described the elder boy as her stepson, so did that mean she had been married before? Had her husband been the father of her children or not? Grimacing faintly at himself for his almost compulsive curiosity about her, Jay turned his attention instead to his surroundings. The dining room had once been elegant, and still bore faded traces of that elegance. The dark red silk wallcovering had faded in places, but still glowed richly, as did the heavy, much polished furniture. A thick Turkey carpet covered the gleamingly polished floor, and Jay found himself reflecting that someone obviously spent a good deal of time and attention on the house. Someone? This tiny, fragile-looking woman, busily placing mats on the table? It must be, at least if Philip was to be believed about her financial status, and he saw no reason to doubt the solicitor.

Whilst he was studying her the door opened and three children trooped in. Charles first, followed by two children so alike that Jay found himself half stunned by them. Two enquiring faces turned speculatively towards him, two identical curly heads angled in his direction.

'Mr Brentford . . . 'please let me introduce you to the children. Charles, you already know, and these two terrors are the twins, Julie and James.'

There was something almost familiar about them, and yet for the life of him Jay could not fathom out what. It was just something that tugged elusively at his memory.

The twins were studying him with a lively curiosity that Vicky regarded with misgiving. Although normally indifferent to their guests, the twins had a propensity for practical jokes that she had not yet been able to make them realise could have an adverse and direct effect on the household income. She would have to talk to them, Vicky recognised despairingly. Jay Brentford, for all his easy smile and calm acceptance of their scrutiny, did not strike her as a man who would tolerate intrusions into the privacy and affronts to his dignity without retaliation.

While everyone sat down she hurried back into the kitchen for the dinner wagon, placing the hot dishes on to the table mats and then giving everyone a warmed plate.

'Please help yourself, Mr Brentford,' she invited coolly. It was disturbing her to have this man seated at the table with them. She had out of necessity placed him at its head, and it was a disturbing sensation to look up and see him seated there. She and Henry had never lived properly together as a family—he had been too ill to eat downstairs in those last months, and the twins had been babes in arms. She and Charles had eaten together, quickly snatched meals—but this was the first time she could ever remember sitting down to a meal in this fashion. Of course their other guests had dined with them when they had only had the odd couple staying, but that was what it had always been—a couple, never a single man, and never, ever a man as masculinely vibrant as this one was.

As he helped himself to food and then passed the dishes back to her Vicky was aware of the twins' open interest in him. Julie was seated on his right hand, watching him intently.

'Julie, get on with your supper,' Vicky instructed her mildly.

'Can we do Christmas cards tonight?' Julie managed to drag her attention away from their lodger long enough to put the question.

'I don't see why not.'

Although she would never have admitted it to a soul, Vicky loved Christmas. She had never really lost her childish thrill in it, and even now with money tight and the children growing bigger every year, she still loved every aspect of it, from writing out the cards, to collecting and decorating the tree. On Christmas Eve last year she had taken all three children to Midnight Mass for the first time. And for the first time that she could remember, when they came out both twins had been completely silent.

'I expect you're getting very excited about Father Christmas.'

Two pairs of contemptuous grey eyes turned towards the head of the table.

'We know there isn't really any Father Christmas,' Jamie told Jay scornfully. 'We *are* nine years old you know.'

Jay felt the full weight of their combined disgust, and hiding a smile apologised easily. 'I'm afraid I'm not really used to children,' he apologised down the length of the table to Vicky. Did that mean he hadn't any of his own? For some reason an alarming mixture of relief and joy pulsed through her at his words, and to stem these totally unwarranted emotions Vicky snapped curtly, 'They aren't exactly some rare breed of animal.'

The twins giggled, and Charles stared at her. It was so unlike her to involve herself in any way with one of their lodgers, never mind snap at them, that she was startled by her own behaviour. Jay Brentford was studying her thoughtfully, one dark eyebrow raised slightly. She was aware that she was at fault and that there had been no need for her to be so curt with him, but the words of apology stuck in her throat. Fortunately, the twins had cleaned their plates, which gave her an opportunity to absent herself. Collecting them she put them on the trolley and headed back for the kitchen.

For dessert she had made a fruit pie from the apples she had carefully stored in the autumn. There was cream to go with it—Mr Eccles at the farm kept her well supplied with dairy produce in return for doing his books. She might never have obtained her economics degree, but she had managed to persevere with her studies long enough to be a reasonably efficient book-keeper and supplemented their meagre income by working for some of the local farmers. It had been Philip who had got her this work, since many of the locals were his clients, and she was conscientious about doing it, not wanting to let him down.

When she got back to the dining room she paused outside the door, astonished by the hubbub of voices coming from inside. When she pushed the door open all sound ceased, until Jamie burst out excitedly.

'Ma . . . guess what . . . Jay is going to take us to get our Christmas tree before he leaves.'

Jay? 'It's all right, I asked them to call me that,' she was informed even as her protest was forming.

'Yes. I was telling him how difficult it was to get

a tree big enough for the drawing room, because
we don't have a car, and the best ones come from
Layer Wood and how you have to go and collect
them yourself . . .'

'Jamie!' she interrupted curtly, flushing with
embarrassment and guilt, knowing that Jamie had
deliberately manoeuvred their lodger into a
position where he had been trapped into offering
his aid whether he knew it or not, but again she
was forstalled.

'Please don't get angry with him, the suggestion
was mine.'

With a killing look at her son that promised
retribution for later, Vicky dished out the pie. Jay
Brentford had cleaned his dinner plate, she
noticed, even though he must surely be used to far
more exotic food than he was likely to get here.
Despite his casual cords and shirt he looked out of
place in the shabby dining room, and simply by
being there made her feel uncomfortable. He was
the sort of man more used to staying at five-star
hotels than shabby boarding houses. Lost in her
own thoughts it was several seconds before
Victoria realised the silence around the table,
engendered she knew by her own sharp reaction to
Jamie's words, and yet conversely, it was Jay
Brentford she blamed for the unusual silence and
not herself. As she rose to clear away the sweet
dishes, she was struck by the uneasy feeling that
somehow he posed a threat not just to her, but to
her whole way of life. Telling herself that she was
being ridiculous she wheeled the trolley back to the
kitchen. No one could affect her life unless she
allowed them to do so, certainly not a man like
Jay Brentford, who was simply a stranger, passing
through. And yet already somehow he had become

involved in the fabric of her life; he had already disturbed her senses to an extent that antagonised and alarmed her; that made her feel vulnerable one minute and resentful the next. The twins had chattered away to him in a manner they never adopted towards strangers—like her they normally held aloof from their lodgers, and even Charles seemed to be showing the incipient signs of a mild degree of hero worship.

'I expect you'd prefer to have coffee in your own sitting room,' Vicky suggested when she returned. She had already arranged a coffee tray for him, reinforcing the determination behind her words. She didn't know what it was about this man that was making her behave in this way, she just knew that for some reason it disturbed her to be close to him.

'Oh, Ma, I wanted to ask Jay about his car,' Jamie protested, and once again Victoria felt herself flush with anger. 'Mr Brentford is here on business, Jamie,' she told her son, stressing the 'Mr'. 'I'm sure he has far more important things to do than to talk to you.' She avoided both Jamie's and Jay Brentford's eyes as she spoke, instead continuing to hold the tray.

Recognising his cue Jay stood up. 'We can talk about the car another time,' he told a disappointed Jamie, taking the tray from Vicky before she could stop him.

'You mustn't let the children disturb you, Mr Brentford,' she muttered as he walked to the door. For some reason he was making her feel guilty, and petty, and it wasn't a feeling she liked.

'Don't worry, Mrs Moreton, I won't,' he responded quietly as she opened the door for him, 'but that's more than I can promise about their mother.'

He said the words so quietly that Vicky could hardly believe she had actually heard them. What was he trying to do? Flirt with her? But there had been nothing remotely flirtatious about the burningly intense way his eyes had met hers and then lingered hotly on her face. Shivering slightly she closed the door behind him.

'That wasn't fair. You made him go away,' Julie protested bitterly. 'We wanted to talk to him.'

'I'm sure you did,' Vicky agreed calmly, feeling much more in control of herself now that his disturbing presence had been removed. 'But like I said, Mr Brentford is here to work and you mustn't pester him.'

'We weren't pestering him,' Jamie argued, his fair skin colouring with resentment. 'We were talking to him.'

'Jamie told him about wanting a BMX for Christmas,' Julie put in earnestly. 'He didn't know what it was . . .'

'That's because he hasn't got any children of his own,' Jamie supplied wisely, for once having the upper hand on his sister. 'I asked him.'

Impossible to stop the swift spurt of pleasure heating her veins. No children didn't mean no wife, Victoria warned herself, and then was aghast by the direction of her thoughts. What was it to her whether he was married or not? Nothing. Nothing at all!

# CHAPTER THREE

'COME on, hurry up, or you're going to be late for the school bus.' The kitchen was in chaos, as it was every morning around this time. The remnants of the children's breakfasts lay on the table. The twins were rushing about collecting school books and sports kit, Charles was pulling on his cycling gear. As she chivied them Vicky glanced anxiously out of the window. The temperature had risen slightly overnight and although it was still freezing, there was an ominous bank of cloud on the horizon that suggested snow.

She had been up since six, attending to her chores; she had taken a breakfast tray into their lodger at eight and left it in his sitting room with a note to use the telephone to ring her if he should want anything more. She knew that he had been up from the sounds of water running in the bathroom, and had had to force down an unwanted and illuminating mental image of him standing beneath the stinging lash of the shower, his body totally male ... strong ... Shaking her head, she wondered a little bitterly what was the matter with her. She never felt like this about men. Never. Well she did now, she told herself grimly, colour flooding her face as the kitchen door opened and the subject of her thoughts walked in.

'Mr Brentford.' The smile she gave him was tight with inner fear and anxiety. He was carrying his tray, which he placed on the table, and like yesterday he was dressed in cords and a shirt, only this time he had a sweater over the top of his shirt. A cashmere one at that, Vicky suspected.

'Look Ma, it's snowing,' Julie screamed excitedly, gazing at the window. Vicky felt her heart sink. She had thought it might and she glanced at the twins' duffle-coated figures, worrying about them keeping warm. It was a long walk to the bus stop for the school bus—nearly half a mile. Charles always went with them and saw them safely on to it before continuing on his bike—his school was in the same direction but a couple of miles further on. The twins' jackets were last year's and too short and tight, but there was simply no money for new ones. Urging them into wellingtons Victoria glanced unhappily again at the window. The snow flakes were fine but coming down fast, and as she knew from experience this part of the Cotswolds was subject to heavy snow and drifts in the winter. Because of their remoteness they were often snowed in, and although she fought not to show any panic she was always frightened that the children would get marooned on the way back from school.

'Come on,' Charles urged. 'You'll miss the bus, you two.'

'Look, why don't I take them to school this morning?'

Victoria stared at their guest. He shrugged lightly. 'I have to go into town to call at the bank and the post office. I'm sure the schools won't be much out of my way.'

Everything in her urged her to refuse him; warned her that it was dangerous to become beholden to this man in any way, and yet how could she deny the children the opportunity to get to school easily and in comfort, just because of her own inexplicable feelings?

Across the room their eyes met over the oblivious heads of the children. Vicky felt her skin flush and a strange heat seemed to invade her body. She felt curiously weak, almost light-headed. She heard her own voice as though it came from far away acceding to his suggestion and then the twins' cries of delight as they rushed about willingly pulling on wellingtons and snatching up scarves and gloves. She was conscious of following them to the door to see them off. Of kissing each childish cheek, even Charles', although he pretended to despise such a childish display of affection, and yet all the time she was aware of something stronger, of something overriding these mundane activities, of a strange sensation of melting heat spreading through her veins, tangling with disturbing mental images of Jay Brentford. Her mouth felt dry and she touched her tongue to her lips. A terse sound from across the room caught her attention. She looked up. Jay was watching her, his gaze fixed on her mouth. Her heart started to beat like a heavy drum, thudding against her ribs, her breath was coming jerkily as though she had just been running.

'I shan't be long.'

Mundane enough words and yet they held the power to make her stomach contract tensely and her face to flood with colour. Long after the sound of the BMW's engine had died away Vicky remained where she was, standing in the kitchen, staring at the back door like someone transfixed.

It was the jarring ring of the telephone that eventually roused her. She picked up the receiver and said the number, tensing when she heard the cool, clipped tones of another woman asking for Jay.

'I'm afraid he's out at the moment.'

'Is he? Oh, well when he comes back will you ask him to ring me. He knows my number, just tell him it's Laine will you?'

Vicky stood numbly where she was when she had replaced the receiver. Jay's caller could be anyone; his secretary, a friend, anyone and yet every instinct she possessed told her otherwise.

Telling herself briskly that she ought to be relieved, that she ought to have known that a man like Jay Brentford was bound to have a woman in his life, she set about the washing up. It was relief that was making her feel so edgy she told herself when she had cleared the table. She had had a lucky escape. God knows why but she had been in distinct danger of being drawn towards the man— she could admit that now, but she had too much pride, too much self-respect to allow herself to be drawn into some form of casual dalliance with a man who she barely knew and who would be moving out of her life in two short weeks. No doubt the Jay Brentfords of this world were well used to the casual sexual alliance but she was not, and she had learned the dangers of indulging in one in the most painful way possible. Her self-respect had been hard won—how hard won only she really knew—and she wasn't about to lose it all for the sake of a few hours of pleasure in the arms of a man who was virtually a stranger. Hot colour burned across her skin as she realised the direction of her thoughts. The wooden table had never been scrubbed so hard as it was now, as though by expending all her energy she could banish the tormenting images from her mind.

What was the matter with her she demanded painfully of herself as she stood up to push wayward curls out of her eyes. Could she only be attracted to strangers; to men with a powerful sexual aura that no woman could deny? An admission she had never allowed herself to acknowledge before slid painfully into her mind. From the outset she had been attracted to the twins' father. She could not remember now what he looked like—or at least only dimly. He had been dark, and virilely masculine—yes, definitely virilely masculine . . . she could well remember even now how her stomach had contracted on a painful surge of desire the moment she saw him. She had been too naïve to recognise that desire for what it was at eighteen . . . too blissfully delighted to have his arms around her as they danced to be aware of what was really happening to her, but now she was twenty-seven—nearly ten years older, but not, it seemed, ten years wiser. A sense of self-disgust flowed through her, and she forced herself to get back to work to blank out the chilling sensations spreading through her veins.

When Jay's car returned she was out feeding the hens. They didn't like the snow, preferring the warmth and comfort of their coop.

Seeing the house for the first time in daylight, Jay was struck by the isolation of it. In the small paddock the snow was already covering the short grass. He could see Vicky, and he stood for a moment watching her. Dressed in faded jeans, wellingtons and a thick sweater she looked little more than a teenager, at least until she stood up and he saw the full curve of her breasts, and the purity of her profile, her curls tangling in the sudden gusting of wind. She was wearing a woollen hat and her cheeks were pink from the cold, her face free of make-up. She was totally unlike any other woman he had met in his life—as different from his normal glamorous girlfriends as chalk from cheese, and yet as he watched her Jay knew that he desired her more than he could remember desiring any other woman he had ever known—except of course Jenny.

Jenny who had been the beautiful role model to which he had hitherto compared all the other women he had desired.

Victoria looked up and saw him watching her. A shiver which had nothing to do with the cold invaded her body. She felt both weak and hot at the same time. He looked so dark and masculine, standing there against the snowy skyline. Across the distance separating them she looked at his mouth and wondered hectically what it would be like to feel it covering her own. The intimacy of her thoughts shocked and angered her. She was like an adolescent held fast in the claws of an intense crush. She barely knew the man and yet here she was going hot and cold with an aching desire for his lovemaking. If it wasn't so frightening it would have been ludicrous. He was coming towards her. Hastily she picked up the hens' bucket, holding it in front of her as though it were a shield. Her action was not missed by Jay and his mouth tightened. What was the matter with him, he wondered irritably? If he had any sense he would welcome her withdrawal from him, the last thing he needed was to get himself involved with a poor widow with three kids to support. It wasn't his style at all.

'There's been a telephone call for you,' Vicky told him as soon as he was within hearing distance. 'Laine ... she said you knew the number.'

So that was why she was being so cool. Mentally cursing Laine under his breath he stood still. Why was it that a grown woman with three children should remind him so poignantly of a timid fawn? He was being over-imaginative he told himself. He had been working far too hard ... but hard work was his *raison d'être* ... the whole purpose of his life. For the first time since Jenny he found himself questioning if that was entirely wise, if there was not after all more to life than acquiring more and more business assets. Like what? he asked himself sardonically as he watched Vicky's remote back as she turned her attention back to her hens. Like a rambling old house, three kids and a woman who made his body react in a way he couldn't remember it reacting in one hell of a long time?

Dismissing the thought as so totally revolutionary as to be unbelievable he headed back to the house. Perhaps it might be as well to speak to Laine. Talking to her would no doubt inject a much-needed dose of reality into life.

By lunchtime the snow was over two inches deep outside the house and still falling, more menacing now to Vicky's experienced eye, heavy, thick flakes that seemed to float relentlessly down out of an ominously pinky-grey sky.

She hadn't seen Jay Brentford since his return, but knew that she could not put off doing so any longer. As his landlady she had to find out if and when he would require lunch.

She was just making for the hall when her 'phone rang. It was the twins' school advising her that they were sending the children home early because of the weather. The school bus would be running, the head-mistress's secretary told her, and the children would be leaving within the hour.

She would have to go down to the bus stop and wait for them Vicky decided as she hurried back into the hall and up the stairs. Outside the door to Jay Brentford's suite she hesitated, trying to quell the panicky sensation of excitement-cum-resentment racing through her veins.

He opened the door as soon as she knocked, his dark hair ruffled, as though he had been running exasperated fingers through it, and his sweater discarded. His thin wool shirt clung to the muscles of his back as he opened the door and then turned away to let her in. A strange weakness seemed to invade her, a sensation so unlike anything she could ever remember experiencing before that she could only simply stare numbly at him when he turned and looked back at her. Her mouth felt dry, her body unfamiliar; vulnerable; her heart was pounding so loudly it seemed to deafen her. Somehow she managed to regain control of her disordered senses. She had obviously interrupted him at his work because the desk was covered in papers; a dictating machine was pushed to one side; a briefcase open on the sofa.

'I'm sorry to interrupt you but I was wondering about lunch.'

'Lunch?' She watched him frown and sensed the formidability of him; aware suddenly of an inflexibility of purpose about him which had no doubt helped him enormously on his journey to success.

I don't normally eat at lunchtime,' he told her at last. 'I prefer to put the energy wasted in digesting food to better use.' She knew that he was referring to his work and yet, at the same time, the way he looked at her started a fast pulse beating hectically under her skin. It appalled her to acknowledge how little imagination she required to picture him making love. The enormity of the intrusion into his privacy of her thoughts shocked her. What was the matter with her? She never, ever reacted to any man like this, never mind a complete stranger.

To cover her confusion she spoke hurriedly. 'I'll just bring you some coffee then and a light salad. I've got to go out to meet the twins off the school bus . . . the weather . . .'

She saw him frowning and bit her lip, telling herself savagely that she was acting like a fool. He didn't want to be burdened with details of her domestic duties. He had come here to work.

'How do you intend to get to the bus stop?' His voice was curt, the unexpectedness of his question startling her. She stared up at him, suddenly mesmerised by the intensity of his grey-eyed concentration on her.

'Walk . . .' How on earth did he think she intended to go there, she wondered grimly.

'In this?' He gestured to the window and his mouth hardened. Vicky suddenly felt as irresponsible and foolish as a schoolgirl and she flushed angrily at the derision in his voice.

'I'll pick them up for you.'

It was more of a statement than a suggestion, and she was completely taken aback by it. 'Really there's no need,' she began stiffly, only to have her refusal swept aside as he came towards her and demanded softly, 'What is it that I've done that makes you so wary of me?'

What on earth could she say? She felt herself

colour up as guiltily as a naughty child. How
could she admit that it was her own awareness of
him that made her feel so tense and nervous?

'I'm not,' she denied stiffly in the end. 'It's
simply that I don't wish to inconvenience you. The
children are my responsibility.'

His gaze narrowed on her face as he caught the
rejection in her voice. 'But presumably a responsibility you have in the past shared with
others?' His voice was as smooth as cream, but still
the tiny hairs on the back of her neck prickled
warningly. 'Charles' father,' he probed, prompting
her, 'and before that their own . . .'

Her chin firmed and tilted, her eyes darkening
to the green of the North Sea in winter as she
faced him. 'The twins never knew their father . . .
nor Charles' come to that, because he died when
they were very young—not that it's any of your
business.'

'Nor is it,' he agreed coolly, half turning away
from her, as though the subject no longer
interested him. She was just starting to relax when
he added softly, 'Is that the reason for the
antipathy I sense in you towards the male sex?
Because you feel that men aren't to be trusted?'

Before she could argue, he went on silkily, 'It is
there you know, no matter how much you might
deny it. You must have been very young when the
twins were conceived.'

'Eighteen,' Vicky told him baldly, too angry and
tense to care what he thought any longer, 'and
before you ask, no, I wasn't married to their
father . . .'

He didn't seem particularly shocked, although
there was a tenseness about him that made her
own defence systems scream out a warning to her.

'Who was he? Another teenager, as unprepared for parenthood as you must have been yourself?'

It didn't strike her to tell him that he had no right to ask her such personal questions—not then; she was too angry for that ... too bitter as old memories churned and surfaced through the tumult he himself had aroused inside her.

'No, he wasn't,' she told him curtly. 'He was a man I met when I was at university.'

'Someone older ... married ...'

'I haven't the faintest idea.' It gave her an unexpected thrill of pleasure to say the rash words and watch his reaction to them. He was good at schooling his features, she had to give him that, but not quite good enough. He was not shocked ... but definitely surprised. She compressed her mouth grimly. Well, let him think what he liked; what did she care?

'The twins were the result of a one-night stand I spent with a man whom I'd never set eyes on before that night,' she told him coolly. 'Now, is there anything else you'd like to know?'

'Yes.' The terse word checked her as she moved towards the door. What on earth was he going to ask her now? Something about Henry? She frowned, and then gasped as he moved, his fingers curling into her upper arms, a febrile glitter darkening his eyes to the colour of wet slate as he stood over her. This close she could smell the male heat of his body; see the dark line of his beard against his jaw.

'What is it?' Somehow she managed to articulate the words, too stunned to even think of pulling away in time as he bent his head and muttered against her mouth, 'This.'

This, was a kiss of controlled savagery that sent

shock waves of reaction juddering all through her
body. She tried to cut herself off from what was
happening, but the hard pressure of his mouth on
her own wasn't something she could easily ignore.
She had been kissed since the twins' conception;
light hopeful kisses that she had managed to keep
under control from men who soon learned that
there was no place for them in her life, but she had
never been kissed with such sexual force before—
never, and it shocked her to the marrow of her
bones to accept how hard it was for her to resist;
how hard she had to fight against the overwhelming pull of her own sexual response. She
wanted this man; wanted him with a physical
intensity that was an ache inside her; a need that
beat at her self-control and threatened to
obliterate it. At last he released her and she was
mortified to discover how much she was trembling.

When at last she felt she had enough self-control
she said grittily, 'If it wasn't for the fact that we
badly need your money I would demand that you
leave right away, and if you ever, ever do that to
me again . . .' Her fingers curled into her palms,
the itch to hit out at him so strong that it took all
her willpower to control it, and she knew even
then that it wasn't really him who she wanted to
hit out at but herself and the sensations he aroused
inside her.

'I've been wanting to do that ever since last
night,' he told her softly, ignoring her bitter words.
'And if you're honest with yourself you'll admit
that you wanted it, too, for all you refused to
respond to me. I'm old enough and experienced
enough to know when a woman desires me,
Vicky.'

'Maybe you are.' She drew herself up to her full

height, trembling as she did so. 'But mere desire, no matter how intense, is not, in my eyes at least, sufficient excuse to jump into bed with somebody, so if that's what you had in mind . . .'

He ignored the last part of her indignant speech to say softly, 'Isn't it . . .? Strange, when you were telling me about the twins I had the distinct impression that it was.'

Too late, Vicky realised where her resentment had led her. With icy coldness she said frostily, 'That was when I was eighteen. People change in ten years.' She stepped away from him. 'I'll go and get your lunch.'

'Don't bother, I'll eat when I've collected the twins. What about Charles, though?'

Vicky bit her lip. She wanted to refuse to allow him to help her, but she had the children to think of. She couldn't let her pride stand in the way of their safety. 'He went on from the twins' school on his bike this morning didn't he?'

'Yes, but he won't be able to ride back on it. Why don't you ring the school and find out if it's closing any earlier, and if it is, I can pick him up and then collect the twins.'

'That's very good of you, but really you needn't bother,' she told him hesitantly, adding defensively, 'Why *are* you doing it?'

'So suspicious,' he mocked. 'Not because I think it will get me into your bed, if that's what you're thinking. Has no one ever done you a kindness before?'

'Henry, Charles' father,' she said quietly. 'He married me, gave me and the twins a home . . .' She glanced at him bewildered by the discovery of how much she had told him about herself. She was normally so reticent.

'And haven't you yourself ever done anyone a small favour?'

She frowned. Of course she had, but ... 'I don't want to be beholden to you ...' she began stubbornly only to stop as he laughed, not with amusement, it was more a sardonic harsh sound than an amused one. 'I already know that,' he told her grittily. 'You've made it more than abundantly clear. Tell me,' his eyes again looking intently at her in that disconcerting manner that he had, 'is it just me that has this effect on you, or men in general?'

'You're a guest here,' she responded sidestepping the issue. 'I don't want to take advantage. I——' She broke off as his 'phone rang. He strode towards it, picking up the receiver, and then turned his back to her as he said, 'Laine, yes. I did ring but you were out.'

Although she knew she ought to leave, for some reason Vicky could not do so. 'Yes. I'll be staying down here for a couple of weeks at least.' There was a pause, and then he said mildly. 'Well, my dear, you must do whatever you think best.' There was another long pause and then he said finally. 'Yes. Goodbye, Laine,' and as she watched him replace the receiver, Victoria was unnervingly convinced that she had just witnessed the end of a relationship, and moreover, that Laine whoever she was had most definitely not been expecting that reaction from him when she had put to him what sounded to Vicky from her position as eavesdropper, suspiciously like an ultimatum.

Stupidly she still could not move, and was unaware that her thoughts were mirrored in her eyes until Jay Brentford drawled mockingly. 'There's no need to look like that. It was hardly the love affair of the century. Laine, I suspect, already has her next victim lined up.' His mouth curled into a humourless smile. 'Shocked? Don't be. Laine was as aware of the limitations of our relationship as I was.'

'You didn't love her?' Vicky was barely aware of mouthing the words, but he must have heard them because he gave her another cynical smile.

'Hardly.'

'And yet you were lovers.'

'Physically yes, but why the shock? I find it a curious reaction in a woman who openly admits that her children were fathered by a total stranger in an act that was apparently not rape.'

He said it so cynically that Vicky could not quite prevent herself from muttering under her breath. 'It might just as well have been.' She sensed he was about to question her further, so she slipped through the door before he could do so, infuriated by the cool, 'Don't forget to ring Charles' school,' that he called after her.

She knew she was acting irrationally; she ought to be grateful for his kindness in collecting the children. Certainly she had been very worried about how Charles was to get home, and yet at the same time she resented him, and not just because of her own sexual response to him, she resented sharing her responsibility for the children with him, however briefly, she realised, surprising herself by the realisation. Could that be one of the reasons she had shunned male company? Did she want to keep the children to herself? Shrugging, she dialled the number of Charles' school, and eventually got through. They *were* sending the children home earlier the secretary told her, and so she asked the woman to pass on a message to Charles to wait there until he was picked up.

Jay came into the kitchen just as she replaced the receiver, and listened calmly while she passed on the information. Looking at him now she found it difficult to imagine that she had been in his arms ... that he had kissed her with that intense sexual need she had sensed in him, and even more difficult to accept how much she had wanted him. She had been the victim of a foolish fantasy she told herself. She was over it now ... his behaviour had shocked her out of it. What did he think she was? Some lonely widow only too eager to throw herself into the arms of any man who offered? Whipping up her indignation she made them both coffee and then pointedly placed his mug on the table while carrying her own over to the window, her back towards him as she sipped the reviving liquid.

'It must be quite a struggle for you to keep this place going.' He had come to stand behind her and instantly she was possessed by a compulsive need to get away from him. Whenever he came close to her she seemed unable to function properly. He was dangerous to her. God alone knew why ... God? She grimaced inwardly; she wasn't *that* much of a fool surely? He was an intensely sexual man; an exciting, magnetic man with just that blend of arrogance and sexuality that aroused an instinctive feminine response.

'It's been in Charles' family for generations,' she answered him, managing to sidestep past him and sit down at the table. 'I promised his father I'd do all I could to pass it on to him. Henry knew he was dying when he married me,' she added simply, talking more to herself now than to him. 'He was a friend of my grandmother's. I told him about my pregnancy and he offered to marry me. It was a bargain we made. He was dying and he wanted to be sure that Charles would be properly looked after. He was a comparatively wealthy man, but before he died he made some unwise investments; he thought he was protecting us all, securing the future for us. But it all went wrong.' She sighed and then stood up. 'But he did marry me. He did give both me and the twins a roof over our heads ...'

'And because of that you feel obliged to keep this place going, is that it?'

'Not entirely. The children enjoy a standard of life here they would never get in a town, which is where I would have to live if I were to find a job that paid well enough to support us all. We might not have much actual cash, but they are well fed, healthy ... they have a degree of freedom that city reared kids can never have. Charles is very adult for his age. I can talk to him about things, although I try not to burden him too much. He knows that keeping this place depends on how well he does in life. He's a clever boy, doing very well at school. He wants to train as a surgeon.'

'A long and costly business.'

'Yes, but I think he can do it. We don't do too badly, especially with the money from the paying guests in summer. Charles comes into a small inheritance from his mother when he's twenty-one; that will help finance his training.'

'And the twins?'

'I don't know,' Vicky frowned. 'It's early days yet ... they're both very intelligent, but inclined to be lazy ...'

'What did their father do?'

He put the question lightly but she was on the

defensive immediately, her cool, 'I don't have the faintest idea,' laced with rejection.

'Don't they ever ask about him?' he asked her suddenly, further unnerving her. 'Aren't they at all curious?'

'Not particularly,' she said it dismissively, standing up as she did so. 'If you really are going to collect Charles, then . . .'

He smiled mirthlessly. 'Very adroit . . . but will you be able to dodge *their* questions as easily, one wonders?'

He had been gone fifteen minutes when the 'phone rang. Vicky answered it. It was Philip Sterne.

'Vicky, my dear.' As always he was avuncularly jovial. 'How are you getting on with Jay Brentford?'

'He seems pleasant enough.' She was guarded, careful about how much she betrayed.

'An extremely clever young man—and a very wealthy one. A trifle hard though. Still I suppose one needs to be to be successful.'

'He's not married then?' Vicky heard herself saying to her own consternation.

'No . . . nor ever has been as far as I know. Unusual that, in these days . . . I really rang to ask if you were free for dinner the week before Christmas Eve. Christine is coming home and she's been asking about you.' Christine was his daughter; the same age as Vicky, and one of her friends from her university days. Christine had been at the party on that fateful night, although neither she nor Vicky had ever spoken of it. But then Christine had probably been too involved with her own boyfriend to notice what she was doing, Vicky reflected.

'Fine, I'd love to come,' she agreed, 'provided I can get a babysitter of course.'

'All organised, Madge will do it.'

Madge was Philip's secretary, a comfortable motherly widow in her late fifties. The children liked Madge and she liked them.

'Okay, you can count me in then,' Vicky told him. She would enjoy seeing Christine again. She had married since Vicky had last seen her, a lawyer from the States. It would be interesting to see how much, if at all, she had changed.

# CHAPTER FOUR

WHEN she had replaced the receiver, Vicky marked the date down on the wall calendar she kept hanging in the kitchen, noticing rather wryly as she did so, all the other blank spaces. It suddenly struck her how narrow and confined her life was; her social commitments were virtually nil, and up until now this was how she had preferred things. It struck her all at once that her lifestyle was rather an unnatural one for a young woman of twenty-seven, and remembering how often she had used the excuse of the children to wriggle out of an invitation she wondered who was really protecting whom. The children did need her, it was true, but they were also quite blessedly independent, especially the twins; she could go out far more than she did if she had wished. But she had not wished. Why? Because she was frightened of a repeat performance of what had happened on the night of that fatal party? Surely she wasn't so naïve?

It struck her as she busied herself in the kitchen that it was Jay Brentford's arrival in her hitherto peaceful and contented life that had given birth to these uncomfortable self-examinations and irrationally she felt a quiver of fear dart through her. So he had reminded her that she was a woman; so she had been sexually aware of him; quite intensely so, well wasn't that a good thing rather than a bad? After her one and only experience of the sexual act she might have found herself unable to respond to the male sex in any way. Quite unaccountably, even though she was completely alone in the kitchen, she felt herself colouring hotly. Snap out of it, she chastised herself, it was ridiculous for a woman of her age to feel so insanely aware of a man who was virtually a stranger to her.

But she wasn't alone in her awareness. He had felt it too ... Jay Brentford was not a boy in his teens and neither was she a young girl any more; by telling her that he was aware of her reaction to him, he was opening the door to something more intimate between them than the simple relationship of guest and hostess, but that intimacy would have nothing permanent about it; it would be an affair such as he had been involved in many times in the past; over as quickly and as brutally as the one she had so recently heard him terminate with his last womanfriend. Could she handle that? Could she give herself to a relationship that she knew at the start would be so ephemeral? Vicky caught herself up angrily. What in the world was she thinking of? Of course she had no intention of becoming involved in an affair with Jay Brentford. Good Lord she didn't even like the man. But she did desire him ... Serpent-like the thought slid into her mind and would not be dislodged. As her hands mechanically performed their routine tasks her mind was totally absorbed by a rush of hitherto unexperienced thoughts. Pausing to stare out of the window at the still-falling snow Vicky tried to shake them off. She wasn't stupid enough to believe that just because her single experience of sex had been unappealing, it meant that all men were the same, but the truth was that she had been so busily engrossed in providing for her small

family, in keeping them all together, and, in the
early years, simply in the never-ending mechanical
tasks of caring physically for two small babies and
a lonely little boy trying to come to terms with the
death of his father, that there simply had not been
the time or the energy to think about her own
sexuality. That it should so suddenly have forced
itself upon her notice in so demanding a way was a
shock it was true, and she was very wary of
allowing herself to become involved with Jay
Brentford in any way. He was so totally different
from the men she normally met; wasn't that
perhaps one of the reasons she was so attracted to
him; the lure of the unattainable?

But he *wasn't* unattainable; at least not sexually;
he had made that more than clear. What would it
be like being made love to by him? For the first
time the extent of her own inexperience struck her.
Hysterical laughter bubbled unsuppressed into her
throat, filling the silence of the kitchen with the
sound. Who on earth seeing her in her normal
everyday life would guess at the truth? She was the
mother of twins; the stepmother of a teenager; and
the widow of his father.

The twins! She sat down rather heavily in one of
the kitchen chairs, shivering slightly as she
remembered Jay Brentford's comments about
them and their father. How on earth would she
ever be able to tell them that he had been a man
whose memory she hated; that she could not even
remember his face; only the hard demand of his
hands on her body; the shaming knowledge that to
him she had never been a real person, simply a
body he had been using to expiate some deep
resentment against her whole sex. Oh yes, she was
old enough and wise enough now to be able to

recognise that, even if she hadn't been able to do so at the time. It had not been her he was possessing with that fierce anger that had made the experience so painful and degrading for her ... it had been womankind in general. And hate his memory though she did, she did not place all the blame on him. She had gone with him willingly enough, hardly aware of what she was doing after the effect of so potent a drink. No. She was not blameless of what had happened ... She moved uncomfortably on the chair suddenly remembering how she had felt when she had danced with him in the smoky dark atmosphere of the crowded room. Her body had tingled then with the same awareness she now experienced with Jay Brentford ... In her innocence she had been thrilled and excited when his arms tightened round her. Joyfully she had responded to the unspoken invitation of his body. No wonder he had been so abrupt and uncaring with her, Victoria reflected tiredly. No doubt to him she had been the epitome of her generation, willing and eager to take what the night offered; why really should she blame him for taking advantage of all that she had so foolishly offered. Why, indeed? Except that as she remembered he had been older than anyone else there ... old enough surely to recognise that she was drunk and to make allowances for it? But why should she have expected a stranger to protect her from herself? Re-living the past was a pointless exercise; what was done was done. She had never told anyone other than Henry what had happened on the night of the party. By the time her pregnancy had become obvious she and Henry were married. She knew it was the generally held impression in the village that she had got herself into trouble with some boy at university, and she had never denied it. The twins had been born early—five months after she and Henry were married, but what gossip there had been had quickly died—she wasn't the first girl to bring such trouble on herself was the general view of the village, and nor would she be the last.

The sound of a car turning into the drive broke into her thoughts. Jay Brentford and the children were back.

The twins came racing out of the car, kicking up flurries of thick fluffy snow. Jay and Charles followed more slowly behind them, apparently deep in conversation. So intense was her awareness of him as he stepped into the kitchen that initially she was unaware of Charles' hesitation.

'Ma . . .' The mixture of hesitation and pleading in his voice caught her attention and she looked across at him. Clutched in his arms was a small, bedraggled puppy of indeterminate breed, soulful brown eyes gazing back at her.

'We found him by the side of the road,' Charles told her, not letting her speak. 'We took him to the police station and they said that he had probably been left there deliberately. We could have taken him to the animal refuge but they only keep them two days.'

Vicky knew what she was being asked before the words were said. The old labrador she had inherited from Henry had died several years ago, and since then they had not had a dog. This one, to judge from the size of his paws, was going to be quite large. He had a good deal of collie in him, plus, to judge from his coat, a generous helping of alsation. She was conscious of three pairs of eyes fixed earnestly on her face.

Both the puppy and Jay Brentford looked the other way.

'He'll have to be house-trained,' she warned them, 'and a strict rota organised for walks.'

The relief and pleasure shining out of Charles' face was its own reward. She was constantly reminding herself that Charles needed more from her than the twins; that they, to some extent, were self-sufficient, whereas Charles stood alone. He had never known his own mother and the bond they shared went very deep. Often she worried about placing burdens on him that were far too heavy for his immature shoulders. He never seemed to laugh as much as the other two.

'Hooray . . . we've got a dog . . .' Jamie cheered, and she checked him quickly, saying,

'He's Charles' dog, you two and you'd better remember that.'

'But I was going to train him to do real tricks,' Jamie protested.

'Only if Charles lets you,' Vicky told her son firmly. 'A puppy needs to know who is his real master. It would be too confusing for him otherwise, I expect Charles will let you help him out though . . .'

It brought an unfamiliar lump to her throat to see the pleasure shining out of her stepson's eyes. It would do him good to have something that was his very own, she reflected, taking the puppy from him and studying it with wry eyes. There was no doubt about it, the animal was going to be huge, and to judge from the heavy weight of it, no doubt exceedingly clumsy, but there was trust in the beguiling brown eyes, and there was something distinctly pleasurable about holding the fluffy warm body.

'First we'll have to take him to the vet,' she warned Charles as the twins started squabbling amicably in the background about who was the better equipped to train him. 'He'll need to have some shots and a check up. We'll need to get him a bowl and a collar and lead. I can get those in the morning when I go into Camwater.' Every other Thursday she made the long trip on the bus to the small market town to buy their staple necessities. It was a chore she loathed; extremely time consuming and depressing in view of how much so few items cost. This week it would be even worse, she reminded herself, because she would have to stock up for Christmas—and do some Christmas shopping.

Because large outlays of money were never possible she normally started preparing for Christmas in August, buying a couple of presents at a time. Christmas had always been a special time of year to her as a child and she did her best to ensure that it was for Charles and the twins. It was heartbreaking to have to explain to them that expensive presents were out, but fortunately they always took it well. Last year Charles had bought the twins and herself presents from the money saved from his paper round. A frown touched her forehead. She didn't want Charles to grow up burdened by the responsibility of the twins. He was a serious boy ... very much the man of the household and the twins occasionally took advantage of that fact.

'Mrs Meadows says that if the snow doesn't melt, we can't go back to school,' Julie announced, digging into her schoolbag. 'She sent you a note.'

The envelope was suspiciously grubby and open at one corner. A lecture on the moral wrongness of opening other people's mail was plainly called for Vicky reflected as she opened and scanned the note. As Julie had said the headmistress deemed it wise to close down the small village school until the weather had improved.

'That means we'll miss the school party on Friday,' Julie complained.

Jamie grinned. 'I'm glad, I hate parties . . . and dancing . . .'

'That's because you know Mary Johnson will kiss you,' Julie retorted, gleefully as she watched her brother squirm. 'She's in love with Jamie,' she told her audience. 'She wants to marry him.'

Jamie's scowl deepened. 'Girls,' he enunciated in tones of deep disgust. 'I'm never going to marry one.'

'You'll never get the chance if you don't get on with your homework,' Vicky intervened drily. 'Come on, books out.'

'But, Ma, we wanted to play out in the snow . . .'

She glanced outside. It was still early, and although she liked all three of them to keep to a routine with their schoolwork, she judged that just this once it wouldn't do them any harm to have a break.

'All right, but only for half an hour, then it's down to work before tea.' The puppy, who was on the floor, suddenly started to make small squeaking noises.

'Charles, I think your new hound is trying to tell you something.' She had almost forgotten that Jay Brentford was still there until he spoke, bending to sweep up the small bundle and open the back door at the same time.

All three children followed it outside, and left

alone with him Vicky was suddenly, and very vividly, reminded of the way he had kissed her. Her body went hot, her heart pounding unevenly inside her chest.

'I hope you don't mind about the pup. Once Charles had seen him I could hardly leave it there to die.'

'No, of course not,' she spoke automatically. 'I think it will do him good to have something of his own. The twins have each other and . . .'

'And?' he prompted softly closing the back door and coming towards her. 'And what do you have, Mrs Moreton? What is there in your life to sustain and uplift you?'

He was taunting her, she could hear it in his voice and anger suddenly speared through her. 'My children,' she told him coolly, stepping away from him. Was he really vain enough to think that she would find an affair with him sustaining and uplifting? Hardly. A small bitter smile curled her mouth. Certainly it would be sexually satisfying, but mentally? Emotionally?

She was glad of the interruption provided by Julie when she came rushing back in to retrieve the gloves she had left on the table.

'An attractive pair,' Jay commented once she had gone, apparently quite content to allow the previous conversation to lapse. 'Both extremely independent though. Do they get that from you or their father?'

'Neither,' Vicky replied, glad that she was able to turn away from him so that he would not see her face. 'I suspect it's because they're twins. They're much closer to each other than they are to me.'

'You've done a good job with all three of them.'

His comment startled her and she swung round,

just in time to catch the hint of surprise darkening his own eyes, as though he too found his remark startling. Vicky sensed that he was not a man who ever involved himself in other people's affairs, preferring to remain aloof and detached and yet he was being remarkably good with all three children.

'The twins as you say are self-sufficient, but that sort of self-sufficiency only comes from being emotionally stable and secure. Charles is more sensitive and in fact, if I didn't know the truth, it would be easier to believe that he was your natural son and the twins your stepchildren.'

'He needs more from me . . .' She said it simply and quietly.

'Yes.' Thick lashes suddenly shielded his eyes as though he didn't want her to see what was in them. 'Do you resent the twins because of their father?'

It was the first time anyone had asked her such a question and it shocked her. 'No, of course not.' The denial was automatic and genuine. She loved the twins fiercely and despite the exasperation their seemingly inexhaustible supply of energy sometimes caused her, was desperately proud of them.

'You're a very unusual woman, Victoria Moreton.' He said it softly, the smile curving his mouth making her stomach turn weak and her blood heavy.

To combat the insidious pull he had on her senses she snapped sharply, 'Why? Because I wasn't willing to jump into bed with you?'

The smile was gone, a hard look of derision replacing it. 'You may not have been willing, but that doesn't mean you didn't want to,' he told her sardonically.

His self-assurance bit into her self-control and she flared hotly. 'And what sort of state would the world be in if we all gave in to every single desire we experience without counting its cost?'

'And what cost would there be in you and I being lovers?' He was watching her closely, too closely, and she suddenly decided that it was better and wiser simply to be honest.

'None probably, if I could be sure that we could be without any emotional involvement, but I'm not so sure that that's possible.'

'And on whose part do you fear this emotional commitment? Mine or your own?'

Why on earth had he asked her the question? He surely must already know the answer. Why should she be concerned about *his* emotions? She already knew they didn't exist. Hadn't she just that morning witnessed the way he ended his affairs?

'My own.' She said it curtly, adding pointedly, 'And if you will excuse me, I really must get on. Supper will be at five-thirty unless you wish to eat later?'

She saw the amusement in his eyes and shivered slightly, wondering what he was thinking. She had hoped by being honest and open with him to make him see that there was no further point in pursuing her.

The last thing a man like him would want was the threat of an emotionally clinging woman. He was old enough and experienced enough to back off at the first hint that she might become one. She need not fear anything from him any more.

But what about yourself, a small inner voice demanded, as he left the room. Was she safe from herself; from her own emotions and responses?

At five-thirty, she herded the children into the

dining room and went back for the heated trolley. Although their meals were simple she always took care that they were attractively presented and that the children learned all the refinements of civilised dining. When she came back with it there was no sign of Jay at the table. She thought about sending one of the children to tell him that the meal was ready and then reflected that it was really her duty to go herself.

It only took her a couple of minutes to reach his rooms. She knocked briefly and then waited until she heard his laconic, 'Come in.'

She pushed open the door, walked into the room and then froze. He was standing in the doorway between his bedroom and the small sitting room. The upper half of his body was bare and in fascination Vicky felt her glance slide the breadth of his chest and then down over his torso, absorbing the total maleness of his body.

'I came to tell you that supper is ready.'

Her voice sounded rusty and unfamiliar, her throat so dry that it felt almost sore. He walked back into the bedroom and then returned pulling on his shirt, unfastening his cords to tuck it in. Almost as though she were moving through water, slowly and clumsily Vicky forced herself to turn her head and look away, her heart was thudding like a sledgehammer, heavy, painful blows that impeded her breathing.

Her legs were trembling badly and for one moment the sensation of terrible weakness spreading through her was so strong that she thought she might actually faint. It took the shock of Jay's fingers biting into her shoulders to drive the giddiness away. His face was pale, his eyes dark, slumberous almost; her heart seemed to

miss a beat as she read their unmistakable
message.

'How long has it been, Vicky?' One hand left her
shoulder, his fingers touching her jaw, stroking the
delicate skin until her muscles quivered with the
effort of not responding to him; of not turning her
face into his hand and seeking more from him
than the tantalisingly slow drift of his fingers
against her skin.

The strange, inarticulate cry she made contained
a need that even she recognised, and burned to
have revealed; she tried to pull away but Jay was
holding her too tightly, and too closely she
recognised as he dismissed the small distance
between their bodies, his hand moving from her
shoulder to her waist, pinning her against him. She
could feel the heavy thud of his heart; her eyes
were level with his throat. The dark smoothness
of it intoxicated her—she wanted—swallowing
painfully she reached out and touched him, her
fingers trembling against the satin skin of his
shoulder. 'Don't do it! Don't do it . . .!' The
warning rang soundlessly through her mind, but
she ignored it, letting it melt in the heat of her
searing response to him.

'Vicky?' There was something almost gentle
about the way he said her name, his breath warm
and sweet against her face as she tilted it up to
receive his kiss.

Slowly and gently, as though they relished the
task, his lips explored hers, mobile and warm, their
touch was a spell that shut out everything else. She
was trembling in his arms, Vicky recognised
muzzily, trembling on the brink of a chasm of
sensation so deep that it frightened her. She tensed
and as though he sensed how torn she was between

wanting to run and wanting more, so much more than the heady touch of his mouth against hers, his grip on her tightened, his tongue stroking her lips.

Desire, intense and all-consuming, possessed her, racing through her veins like raw spirit. Her mouth opened under his, pleasure exploding inside her. His body was hard against her own; hard and unmistakably aroused. A hitherto totally unknown sensation kicked her in the stomach, releasing a storm cloud of sensual flutters. His hand cupped her breast and suddenly she was aching for him to touch her without the hindrance of jumper and bra. She wanted his hands on her bare skin, his mouth . . . The shock of all that she wanted from him made her tense, and as she stepped back to stare at him with stunned eyes, barely able to comprehend what had happened, she heard him answer his own question, his voice soft and silky as he murmured, 'To judge from that I'd say it's been one hell of a time.'

She didn't even realise she'd slapped him until she saw the dull red marks of her fingers against his skin, and the knowledge that he could drive her to such a physical and emotional frenzy made her stomach twist in tight knots of anxiety. What was happening to her? She backed towards the door shakily, her face white and stained. Was *that* how he saw her? As a frustrated young widow, only too eager to welcome the advances of any passing male? The thought shamed and sickened her. How could she humiliate herself further by revealing the truth? That he was quite simply the only man in ten years who had made her remember what it was like to be a woman?

'Victoria.' His voice stopped her by the door. It

was hard, laced with an anger he didn't bother to hide.

'I'm terribly sorry, Mr Brentford, but I must ask you to leave ... Your money will of course, be returned to you.' She said it tonelessly without looking at him, knowing that for the sake of her own sanity she must make him leave.

'Like hell it will.' He reached her in four strides, kicking the door shut with his foot and then holding her against it so that she had no means of escape. 'You wanted me to kiss you,' he told her brutally, 'and more.'

The assurance in his tone brought shamed colour to her face.

She could not deny it, but she had to protect herself somehow. 'And because of that you think I ... I'm easy game,' she demanded bitterly. If only he would release her, even now with every reason in the world why it should not, her traitorous body was intensely aware of him ... of the nudity of his torso beneath his still open shirt ... of the scent and maleness of him.

'Did I say so?' He was watching her closely, the grey eyes still dark, he moved his head and she ached to press her lips against the smooth line of his throat, to melt into his arms and dismiss everything other than her need to be close to him ... part of him.

'By your behaviour you implied it.' Somehow she managed to make her voice cool and remote.

'Because I kissed you?' His mouth was wry, 'Or is it because you kissed me back that you're getting so worked up? And you were, weren't you?' he demanded softly, forcing her to look up at him.

Vicky knew he wasn't talking about her losing

her temper and slapping him and she almost hated him for revealing her weakness.

She managed a small shrug. 'It was only a kiss . . .'

'No, it damned well wasn't. You know it and I know it too. Face up to it Vicky, there's something between us that both of us are aware of. I don't think of you as "easy game", as you call it,' he added quietly. 'Quite the contrary; you're the most prickly and defensive female I've met in a long time. It takes more than simply responding to a man's mouth and hands to make a woman that,' he told her, 'and believe me I know.'

Her eyes slid away from his and she started to tremble. 'I didn't want this . . . I . . .' She shook her head slowly, 'I shouldn't be telling you any of this.'

'Why not? It means that I'm special . . . important even. I like that. I like it very much.' His mouth touched hers and she knew she was lost.

'Ma?' The anxious sound of Charles' voice from the other side of the door brought her back to reality. Jay released her and opened the door at the same time.

'It's my fault your mother's been delayed, Charles,' she heard him saying as she ran anxious fingers through her hair. 'I wasn't ready for supper and I kept your mother talking.'

He was fastening his shirt as he spoke, his actions so matter of fact and commonplace that they tore at Vicky's heart. How many times had he performed this small intimacy in some woman's company before? More often than he could remember no doubt. 'It's snowing again,' Charles announced, lingering by the sitting room door as

Vicky walked towards it. 'Do you think we'll have a white Christmas?'

Thinking of the time still to elapse before the end of December, Vicky found herself praying not. It would be impossible to get out of the house if the weather worsened much more, and she still had so much to do.

'Ready?' Jay was dressed and standing by the door, and it struck her as the three of them went downstairs that they might have been any quite ordinary family unit. The pain that came then was so sharp and intense that she actually winced from it. What a ridiculous thought; they were not a family and never could be.

She was still trying to puzzle out her own thoughts when they sat down to eat. She had never once since Henry's death ever wanted a man to lean on; a husband to share her bed; a father for the children and yet here she was, visualising in that role a man she barely knew . . .

'We've got algebra tonight,' Julie announced gloomily breaking into her thoughts. 'I hate it.'

'That's because you never get it right,' Jamie interrupted loftily, 'and that's because you're a girl.'

The squabble that then broke out was inevitable, and Vicky hastened to put a stop to it. When both twins lapsed into a sulky silence Jay said calmly, 'Why don't I give you a hand with your algebra, Julie, umm?'

Watching her small daughter's face light up and witnessing the coquettish smile she gave him, Vicky could only wonder at Jay's offer. The first time she had seen him she had been struck by his aloofness; and since then everything he had said or done had reinforced that first impression.

He was a man who lived alone, by choice, and yet here he was willingly involving himself with her family. Why? Not because he thought it would influence her response to him that was for sure. He must by now be in no doubt about that ... So then why? Frustrated paternal desires? Hardly; her mouth twisted, he did not strike her as that type.

And yet an hour later watching his dark sleek head bent over the smaller curlier one of her daughter as he explained to her the ramifications of a maths problem, she was once again tormented by the apparent domesticity of the scene. Domesticity and Jay Brentford? It would be like mixing oil with water, and yet there was a calm patience about the way he answered Julie's questions that whispered treacherously to her that he would make a good father.

'You've never wanted children of your own?' The question was out before she could silence it, posed while Julie's attention was elsewhere.

'Once.' Shadows danced in the firelight and a fresh pain struck through her body as she looked at his shuttered face. 'A long time ago.'

'What happened?' Her mouth was dry and stiff.

'She decided to marry someone else. It was a long time ago and very much for the best. However, these things do tend to leave scars.'

'You still love her?'

'No, but the breaking of our engagement isn't a time I like to look back on or to talk about. There are painful associations that even now ...' He broke off as Julie suddenly demanded his attention. What did he mean, Vicky wondered, and then berated herself for wondering at all. What concern was it of hers? He was a stranger, merely passing through her life; a man she desired, it was true, but that was all.

Julie had finished her homework and wanted to watch television. Jay excused himself saying that he, too, had work to do. When he had gone, Vicky got out the accounts she was working on. They were for a farmer who lived several miles away and who had very little idea of how to keep his books. He was more than happy to pay Vicky to do the work for him.

It kept her busy for a couple of hours after the children had gone to bed. When at last she lifted her head from the white sheet in front of her, it was aching slightly. She leaned back in her chair, telling herself she was a fool for wishing she could lay her head against the warm smoothness of a male shoulder ... that she could be enfolded in arms strong enough to support her.

Telling herself that she must be suffering from some weird imbalance of hormones she got up and walked into the kitchen to check up on Charles' puppy. He greeted her eagerly, tail thumping. Vicky let him out, dismayed to see how thick the snow was, and not a star to be seen. It was going to be murder tomorrow getting into town and back but somehow she would have to do it.

# CHAPTER FIVE

AT breakfast the twins grumbled noisily about being roused from their beds when there was no school to go to.

Vicky had sent Jay a breakfast tray via Charles, telling herself that it was not really cowardice that made her so reluctant to face him, merely prudence.

Charles was gone longer than she had expected, and when he eventually returned, he looked rather shamefaced. Jay was at his heels carrying his untouched tray which he placed on the table, frowning at her as he did so.

'What's all this about you going in to town on the bus?' he demanded briskly. For all the world as though she were the twins' age rather than an adult, Vicky reflected indignantly, noting the disapproval in his eyes.

As her glance swung to Charles he looked guiltily away and she checked her mounting irritation. She couldn't blame Charles for what had happened, at least not entirely.

'The weather's far too bad for you to think of doing any such thing—I doubt even if the bus will be running.'

Vicky checked a small protest, silencing it quickly, but he must have noticed her dismay because his eyes narrowed watchfully.

'But I've got to go in,' she protested tensely, only realising as the words were spoken that she had no need whatsoever to justify her decisions to

Jay Brentford. He was a lodger in her home dammit, nothing more. Why on earth couldn't he behave the way her other lodgers had behaved, keeping himself to himself and leaving her alone to run her own life?

'Well, if it's that urgent you can come in with me,' he informed her in a clipped voice. 'I've got to make a call at the factory I've just purchased and check over a few things. It's just outside Camwater.'

So Charles had even told him her destination. She swallowed down the angry bile in her throat. Who did he think he was anyway, taking over her life, bullying her, ordering her about, making her feel as no other man had ever been able to make her feel?

The twins had gone quiet and were watching her curiously. Charles still looked guilty and she bit down hard on her bottom lip, realising that her reaction was so out of character for her as far as the children were concerned that they were studying her a little uncertainly. Her heart seemed to miss a beat and then thud heavily. What was happening to her? What was she turning into?

Taking a deep breath she said politely, 'That's very kind of you, but I'm afraid I'm not sure when I'll be ready to leave . . . there's the hens to feed and . . .'

'I'll do that this morning.'

For the first time since she had known him Vicky was ready to curse Charles' willingness to help her.

'There you are,' Jay drawled, plainly amused and showing it. 'Problem solved.' He came towards her, standing beside her whilst he helped himself to a cup of coffee, and before she had time to recover from her bemusement that he should make himself so at home in her kitchen he was murmuring to her, 'I should give in if I were you, unless of course the trip to town was merely a ploy to get away from me.'

Through gritted teeth she muttered back. 'You flatter yourself. The trip as you call it is a bi-weekly necessity. Three children take quite a bit of feeding, in case you don't realise it—and then there's Christmas . . .'

He sat down and drank his coffee, calmly filching a piece of toast from those she had made for the children, and before she could so much as object had engaged the twins in a discussion on the relative merits of various potential Christmas presents. Listening to them Vicky subdued another stab of resentment. He was talking to Jamie about BMXs. It was the boy's dearest desire to own one, and she had spent many painstaking weeks carefully explaining to him why it would be impossible—they simply did not have the money— that was the main reason but she didn't want any of the children growing up feeling that because of a lack of money during their childhood, in adulthood they must be motivated by the need to acquire it. Although she hadn't said as much to her son, she was hoping that by next Christmas there might be a better choice of second-hand bikes available and that she would be able to afford one of these for him.

Julie wanted a pony, and as she sat listening to her pink-cheeked daughter describing to Jay the merits of this longed-for beast, she suppressed another small sigh.

Charles on the other hand was more realistic and it hurt her intensely to know that he was

deliberately not joining in the excited conversation
because he knew exactly how remote the possibility
was of any of them receiving anything expensive.
There was nothing she would have liked to do
more than to go out and get them all exactly what
they wanted but it simply wasn't possible.

'And your mother. What would she like for
Christmas?'

They were all looking at her, the twins excited
and breathless. A tight vice seemed to close round
her heart and she resented Jay more than she had
ever resented him before. It was not simply that he
came from such a vastly different world to their
own; that he was rich, that he was aloof and
unreachable. It was because he was tantalising her
children with the fantasy glitter of delights that
could never be theirs and she hated him for the
bright expectancy in their eyes ... for their held
breath and their belief that somehow the magical
impossible might just happen.

'All their mother wants is a bit of peace and
quiet and enough money to pay the bills,' she
snapped, hating herself the minute the words left
her mouth and she saw the light die out of their
eyes.

She couldn't meet Jay's, and so instead she got
up, bustling about clearing the used dishes off the
table. The twins started to chatter again but in a
more subdued way this time. Charles, who had
already been out with his new puppy, commented
that they had more snow during the night.

'Mm ... that probably means digging my car
out and putting snow chains on it,' Jay commented,
and then added, eyeing the twins. 'Okay who
wants to earn themselves fifty pence helping me to
do it?'

Tears blurred her eyes as Vicky bent over the sink. She knew quite well why Jay had offered them the comparatively miserly sum of 50p; it was because he knew quite well that her pride would revolt against him offering them more. 'Of course,' he added as he walked over to the door, 'there could be a bonus for fast work. I'll go up and get my jacket.'

As he opened the hall door, she found the composure to say huskily, 'You'll need wellingtons. I've still got an old pair of Henry's, they might fit you.'

She still couldn't look at him; still resenting him for the way he had made her feel over the children's Christmas presents, but she didn't realise that Charles was aware of her feeling until he came up to her, picking up a tea-towel and starting to dry the dishes she had washed, his voice low and uncertain as he asked, 'Ma . . . why don't you like him?'

What could she say? It was all too complicated to explain to a sensitive fourteen-year-old already burdened by more responsibilities than he should have to carry.

'I do, Charles.' she gave him a brief smile. 'It's just that I'm not used to having other people tell me what to do I suppose.'

'I'm sorry I mentioned you going in to town.'

His head was bent and she stretched out a hand to ruffle his tow-coloured hair. He was growing so quickly, already as tall as she was herself. 'You did it with the best of intentions, and I expect he's right. The bus probably wouldn't have been running. Pride can be a great handicap, Charles, it nearly always works against us, making us behave in a silly way. You leave that, I'll finish off. I think your new acquisition is trying to tell you he wants to go out.'

'I'll feed the hens now if you like?' he offered.

She smiled at him. 'No. I'll get the twins to do it later when they've helped J . . . Mr Brentford to dig his car out. It will give them something to do whilst I'm out.'

Charles put down the cloth and then said hesitantly, 'It seemed strange at first having him here. I mean he isn't like the others, you know the people who stay in the summer. He's different, more part of us somehow.' He bent his head even further, scuffing the floor with his shoe as he muttered defensively, 'I like having him here. It makes me feel . . . it makes me feel good.' He lifted his eyes to Vicky's face as he said the last few words, and they were dark with a certain defiant reserve.

Inside Vicky felt the shock waves of his remark pound through her, but she managed to conceal it in her face. 'Charles,' she said gently, 'it's only natural that you should enjoy the company of an older man. If your father had lived . . .' She sighed and then said quietly, 'I know exactly what you mean and I'd like to have someone there to lean on too at times, but we can't always have exactly what we want from life.'

'I know,' Charles looked embarrassed again, 'but it would be nice if you got married again wouldn't it?'

Married again? Did Charles genuinely believe that there was a possibility of Jay wanting to marry her? Her heart ached for him. Poor boy, he was doomed to swift disillusionment. He was coming dangerously close to hero-worshipping Jay and because he was so quiet and withdrawn she had not noticed it earlier. Of course all boys needed a man to model themselves on, she knew that, and that was one of the reasons she had been so pleased when Charles won his scholarship. At an all-boys' school he would get the masculine company and example that he could not get at home. But marry again . . .?

'The twins want you to as well,' Charles added awkwardly, further confounding her. 'We often talk about it.'

They did? 'When?'

'Oh often,' Charles said vaguely. 'Long before Jay came . . .'

She was just about to question him further when Jay came back, the twins in tow. All three of them were warmly dressed, Julie clinging possessively to his hand, her small mittened fingers lost in his masculine clasp. Tears pricked her eyes and she turned away quickly, hating her momentary weakness. What on earth was wrong with her? She was becoming ridiculously sentimental; absurdly so in fact. Jay Brentford might want to go to bed with her, but he certainly did not want to become a stepfather to her children!

She watched them all troop outside, Jay wearing Henry's old boots, and then they disappeared, heading in the direction of his car.

Whilst they were gone she finished tidying up the kitchen, found her shopping list, telephoned the farmer whose accounts she had been working on to tell him that they were completed and would be in the post, and then went upstairs to change into something more suitable than her ancient jeans and shirt.

Her wardrobe didn't exactly brim with an exotic choice of clothes, Vicky reflected wryly, pulling it

open, and up until now that had never really
bothered her; hardwearing jeans, T-shirts in
summer and jumpers in winter had proved ideal
wear for her lifestyles, supplemented by the odd
dress and a couple of skirts. Now for some reason
she felt a twist of dissatisfaction as she studied the
barely half-full cupboard. And then telling herself
that she was being a fool she picked up a clean
pair of jeans and a fresh jumper. Even if she had
expensive clothes it was hardly the weather for
wearing them.

Tugging off her top clothes and depositing them
in the laundry basket, she grimaced faintly as she
caught sight of her own reflection in the long
mirror, her rounded breasts filled the pretty chain
store bra she was wearing, emphasising the
neatness of her waist and the slim curves of her
hips. The clothes she wore masked the femininity
of her figure and since she was not in the habit of
studying the shape of her body without them, she
wrinkled her nose rather incredulously as she
looked at herself. She looked more like a doll than
a grown woman she decided sardonically. She had
always wanted to be taller, and in her teens had
greatly envied her taller friends, but more latterly
she had had other things to worry about. Her hair,
a bright mingling of red and gold hung down to
her shoulders and again she grimaced wondering
what on earth she was doing standing gawping at
herself, and why ... She heard a brief knock on
her door and sighed, reaching out for her clothes.
No doubt one of the children wanting something.
A respect of one another's privacy was something
she had taught them all early in life but she had no
qualms about either Charles or Jamie seeing her in
her underwear.

Calling out 'come in,' she sat on the bed, prior to pulling on her jeans.

'I just thought I'd let you know that we've got the car out . . .'

Vicky froze as she heard the familiar male voice and realised just who it was who had entered the room. At first he hadn't been able to see her but now as he rounded the corner of the bed he did so.

Like someone in a dream she felt completely unable to move . . . to do anything other than simply drown in the darkness of the grey gaze fastened on her face. All movement seemed to be suspended, and then as his gaze moved hotly over her briefly clad body an intense surge of desire swept through her; a sensation of need so all consuming that she was stricken by it.

'Vicky . . .?'

She was caught in the dark under-tow of his reciprocal hunger; she could hear it in his voice; see it in his eyes. Somehow she managed to drag her own away and stand up, albeit very shakily.

'I'll be ready in a minute.' Dear heaven what was happening to her? Was she really so sexually attracted to this man that she was willing to forget that she had three children downstairs; that she was willing to forget and forswear everything, simply for the pleasure of knowing his possession? Pleasure! She shook hysterically. How could so simple a word even begin to encompass the fierce hunger inside her for him?

Pleasure was a word to describe something light and frothy; to be enjoyed indolently; it had nothing to do with this savage sensation clawing through her body; this ache that tormented and demanded.

'Vicky I . . .' He was standing close to her now,

his glance burning, scorching her skin when it touched it. Beneath the thin covering of her bra she could feel her nipples swell and harden. She closed her eyes to blot out his image and with it her feelings, and then wished she hadn't as she immediately pictured the darkness of his head against her breast, his mouth ... Shaken by the images tormenting her she opened them again. He was looking at her mouth. With a moan of sheer anguish she backed away from him, willing him to leave her, sinking tremulously to the bed when he did so.

It took her five minutes to find the energy and will power to get dressed. How on earth could she go downstairs and face him now after what she had just betrayed? Vicky had been brought up in a world where women did not openly betray their desire for men. Her grandmother had brought her up in what she considered the correct way for a young girl, which was no doubt why she had been stupid enough to get herself drunk and pregnant. She had been too innocent to protect herself. But she was not innocent any longer.

Lashing herself with mental scourings she pulled on her clothes and then checked. Was it really so wrong to want to be made love to? She was a woman of twenty-seven, unmarried, who could surely please herself what she did with her own body?

But what about the children? To involve herself in an affair would mean using a considerable amount of secrecy ... And yet she wouldn't be the first woman to conceal her sexuality from her offspring. Biting her lip, she combed her hair, remembering to coat her lips with a protective wind-screen. They glowed softly, fuller surely than normal?

She wanted Jay Brentford; she had to admit that now ... wanted him with a need and intensity that went far beyond anything she had ever imagined herself feeling, even as a romantic teenager. And he wanted her ... but whatever there was between then could only be fleeting. So? She didn't love him. She had no emotional attachment to him. What she felt for him was a physical arousal only. Somehow that made her feel better; stronger; as though she still retained some control over herself; as though there was some part of herself aloof from him.

By the time she eventually joined him downstairs she had herself virtually under control As she pulled on wellingtons and collected a woolly scarf and hat to add to her gloves she was able to face him with a commendable degree of equanimity. Instructing Jamie and Julie to behave themselves and to listen to whatever Charles told them, she allowed Jay to escort her out to his car.

As she slid inside it and buckled on her seat belt, she forced herself to appear composed. Jay, fortunately, was concentrating too much on his driving to pay any attention to her. There were one or two anxious moments before the chains began to bite into the thick snow but at last they were out on the road and on their way.

They had travelled several miles before he spoke and then only to comment on the overcast nature of the sky.

'Looks like there's a good deal more snow up there,' he told her.

Vicky could only agree, and she prayed that it would hold off long enough for her to get her shopping done.

'I think we should try to get back as quickly as

possible,' Jay remarked, echoing her own private thoughts. 'It doesn't look too promising. I shouldn't have to spend too long at the factory—it's just a courtesy visit, really, to make the acquaintance of the staff and to collect some papers I need, so I should be through by lunch-time.

Mentally calculating what she had to do Vicky told him that so should she.

'Good. I'll drop you off in town—the factory is just the other side of it. Where should I pick you up?'

Telling herself that it was ridiculous to be disappointed by his business-like attitude, when not so very long ago she had been telling herself that that was exactly what she wanted from him and no more, she suggested that they meet in the foyer of the town's one and only hotel, which was close to the shops and had the virtue of a large car-park.

'Yes, I know where it is,' Jay confirmed, and apart from making one or two comments about Christmas and what the children wanted for presents there was no further conversation between them until he stopped in the main street of the small market town to let her out.

'The Bells then no later than one o'clock,' he reminded her before driving off again.

Telling herself that it was ridiculous to feel so forlorn Vicky trudged first in the direction of the bank where she had bills to pay and money to draw out. Her next port of call was the town's one and only toy shop where she checked that the things she had had put by for the children at the beginning of the autumn were ready to be collected once she had paid the final instalment on them. Whilst not operating a credit scheme the couple who ran the shop had been willing to put things on one side for her and allow her to pay something towards them on a monthly basis, which made it far easier for her to budget. As she passed a new computer shop which had opened in the high street she looked hesitantly into its window, wishing that it was possible to get Charles one but they were way way beyond her meagre resources. Sighing faintly she pressed on in the direction of the supermarket.

Going there was a chore she hated, just as she loathed having to compare brands and prices, but such economies were necessary, even though they might be time consuming. By the time she had finished there she was alarmed to see that it was snowing once more. Her provisions were all boxed, and for 50p one of the teenagers who helped out at the supermarket was more than willing to push them over to the hotel for her in a trolley and stack them there whilst she waited for Jay. It was just gone twelve o'clock and there was nothing more she had to do other than to call at the post office for stamps. With a bit of luck she might just have time for a coffee before they started back.

As luck would have it there was a long queue in the post office and it was ten to one before she could leave. It dismayed her to see how much snow had fallen in that short time and it was still coming down. Already the main road through the town was white, and traffic had slowed down to a crawl and to judge from the heavy dark sky, there was little chance of the snow abating.

She had been waiting impatiently in the hotel foyer for ten minutes before Jay arrived, too tensed up by the sudden downturn in the weather to bother with a coffee. He came in brushing thick white snow flakes from his jacket, his forehead pleated in a frown.

He saw her straightaway and came over to her. 'Are you ready to leave?' she questioned him anxiously, 'I'm worried about the weather.'

'Yes.' His voice was terse. 'But I'm afraid we might have a problem. There was a weather bulletin on the radio as I drove in. It seems likely that the road out to your place is already blocked.' He saw her panic and grasped her arm. 'Look. Let's get ourselves a cup of coffee and ask someone if they've got a radio here that we can listen to ... or if there's a local centre we can telephone to check up.'

Although she knew this was sensible advice Vicky was filled with a panicky desire to rush out into the snow and walk home if necessary; she was so concerned about the children.

'Don't panic ... Charles is with them,' Jay reminded her, stunning her with his ability to read her mind. 'They're sensible enough kids at bottom.'

She knew he was right, and allowed herself to be led into the coffee lounge. They had to wait some time to be served because it was so full and to judge from the snatches of conversation she heard around her, they weren't the only ones to be concerned about the weather.

Once they had been served Jay disappeared, telling her that he was going to see what he could find out. He came back within minutes his face grim. The road to the Old Vicarage was definitely closed, he told her, not just by the snow but also by a couple of vehicles which had run into difficulties and had been abandoned by their drivers.

'They doubt that they'll get it open before morning—they can't even start at the moment until the snow stops; apparently they're keeping the snow ploughs for the roads that are still open.'

Tomorrow? Vicky stared at him. What on earth were they going to do? 'I tried to get us a couple of rooms here, but they're fully booked,' he added tersely. 'Apparently we aren't the only ones to be stranded. Have you any friends in town? Anyone you could stay with?'

Numbly Vicky shook her head. She did have friends but they all lived outside the town itself.

'The children,' she said weakly, 'I must ring them, I . . .'

'Yes, but not from here. Have you finished your coffee?' When she nodded, Jay called for the bill, and as she followed him back to the foyer and saw the queues forming by the two public telephones, she could understand his comment.

'Is this your stuff?'

In her panic she had forgotten about her shopping, but now nodded her head as he indicated the neatly stacked boxes.

'Let's get them into the car.'

He was the one who had done all the work, Vicky reflected numbly several minutes later as he snapped the boot lid closed, and joined her inside the car.

As he set it in motion she managed to come out of her numbness for long enough to ask, 'Where are we going, we . . .'

'Don't panic,' he drawled laconically, 'I'm not abducting you.' The traffic through the town was nose to tail, and yet despite that the road was still white and the snow getting deeper. Watching other cars skid and bump, she shivered gratefully inside the protection of Jay's, wondering a little at her instinctive trust in him as a driver.

When he eventually turned off at some traffic lights and then down a road which she knew led to the old part of the town she glanced at him in bewilderment.

'It's all right. Ah yes . . . here we are.' He drew up outside an elegant terrace of Georgian town houses and stopped the car.

'When I bought the business, it included one of these houses. It had been bought by the previous owner for his son, and when the business went into liquidation the liquidator took it over. That's what happens,' he added dryly, seeing her face, 'when businessmen get too clever and try to use company funds for private purchases.'

'If you own a house here, then why did you need lodgings?' Vicky heard herself asking stupidly.

'Because I don't like looking after myself, and since I could not get into a local hotel . . .'

'I was the only choice . . .'

'And a rather good one as it turned out . . .' The smile he gave her made her body tremble.

'Luckily I've got the keys; they were handed to me with the spare set for the factory. I believe the place is furnished. I expect it will be cold and probably damp, but at least it will be preferable to spending the night in the car. It also has a telephone so you should be able to ring home and soothe those maternal fears . . .'

The mockery in his tone stung and she swung round saying fiercely . . . 'Those children are my responsibility, of course I'm worried about them. Naturally I don't expect a single man such as yourself to understand that.'

'Why not?' His mouth was grim. 'Do you really

think I'm so feckless and uncaring that I view the thought of them being left alone without a qualm? His eyes held hers and hers were the first to drop. 'However, since there's nothing we can do about it short of hiring a helicopter and dropping down on them—and even then it's doubtful that we could find a pilot idiotic enough to take us—oh yes,' he told her grimly, 'it had crossed my mind, but unlike you I have sufficient faith both in Charles and the twins to believe they have enough responsibility to behave sensibly.

'Come on ...' He got out of the car, leaving her to fumble distractedly with her seat belt. The nerve of the man; with a few well-chosen words he had reduced her to the status of fussing mother, and yet at the same time had chided her for not believing that he too was concerned. Why on earth should he be; they weren't his children? Good heavens, her clumsy fingers stilled ... was she actually jealous of the relationship he seemed to have built up with the children? Did she genuinely in some way feel threatened by the rapport that seemed to exist between them? But why? He was a temporary—a very temporary—fixture in their lives.

'Having problems?' He was standing by her open door watching her and as she shrugged, he made a small sound of exasperation and bent to release her from the confines of her seat belt. Their fingers tangled and white hot sheets of sensation spread through her body from the brief contact. She drew away as though she'd been burned, but when she risked a look at him expecting to see taunting mockery in his eyes, instead they were very dark, highly charged with some emotion she could not understand.

He turned away from her, his mouth tight, his
body tense. Slowly she followed him up the steps
that led to the front door, waiting as he tried
several keys before finding the right one.

As she stepped into the house she reflected that
it was cold ... but there was no trace of damp.

'Kitchen first,' Jay instructed tersely. 'They've
obviously got central heating,' he gestured to the
radiator, 'let's see if we can get it on.'

They could, or at least he could, Vicky reflected,
standing watching as he tampered with the boiler
and eventually got it lit.

'Now, telephone.'

What on earth had happened to her? Vicky
wondered as she docilely followed him from room
to room in search of that instrument. They
eventually found it in the small drawing room. Jay
was the one who picked it up, his forehead
smoothing in relief as he held the receiver to her
and she heard the dialling tone.

'At least it's not been cut off. Okay, you ring the
kids whilst I have a scout round. There's an open
fire in here, with a bit of luck we might be able to
find something to burn in it and boost the
heating.'

Win "Instantly" right now in another way

# ...try our *Preview Service*

Get **4 FREE** full-length Harlequin Presents books

*Plus* this handy, compact umbrella (a $10.00 retail value alone)

*Plus* a surprise free gift

*Plus lots more!*

Our love stories are popular everywhere...and WE'RE CELE-BRATING with free birthday prizes—free gifts—and a fabulous no-strings offer.

Simply try our Preview Service. With your trial, you get SNEAK PREVIEW RIGHTS to eight new HARLEQUIN PRESENTS novels a month—months before they are in stores—with 10%-OFF retail on any books you keep (just $1.75 each)—and Free Home Delivery besides.

THERE IS NO CATCH. You're not required to buy a single book, ever. You may even cancel Preview Service privileges anytime, if you want. The free gifts are yours anyway, as tokens of our appreciation.

It's a super sweet deal if ever there was one. Try us and see.

---

*EXTRA!* Sign up now-—automatically qualify to WIN THIS AND ALL 1986 "Super Celebration" PRIZE & PRIZE FEATURES...or **watch for new prizes and new prize features NEXT MONTH at your favorite store.**

Harlequin
"Super Celebration" Sweepstakes

901 Fuhrmann Blvd.
P.O. Box 1325
Buffalo, NY 14269

PLACE
1ST CLASS
STAMP
HERE

# CHAPTER SIX

CHARLES answered the 'phone on the second ring, sounding relieved to hear her voice. He explained that they had heard about the road being blocked on the radio and that he had been concerned that theirs might be one of the cars stuck in the drifts.

Quickly explaining to him that she would be spending the night at a house Mr Brentford owned in the town, she felt a lump forming in her throat as he said manfully, 'Don't worry about anything here, Ma. We'll be okay.' She was just giving him careful instructions about what to have for their evening meal when Jay walked back into the room, miming to her that he wanted to speak to Charles himself.

Having assured herself that Charles had understood her careful instructions she handed the receiver over to Jay.

He spoke matter of factly and reassuringly to Charles, explaining that he hoped that the roads might be cleared by morning but that just in case they were not they were not to worry because he was sure the snow ploughs would be set to work on it just as soon as they could. He then had a few words with both twins, some comment one of them made making him grin, before he handed the receiver back to Vicky.

'Now you two must both do what Charles says,' she warned Julie. 'He's the eldest.'

When she had finally replaced the receiver, the silence in the room unnerved her. Jay was watching her closely and to break the tension between them she said without thinking. 'What were you smiling about before on the 'phone?'

He grinned again and the look in his eyes further alarmed her. 'Julie was just reminding me that you have no nightclothes with you. She suggested it might be a good idea if we slept together to keep warm. Apparently she picked the idea up from some sort of survival programme.'

To save her life Vicky couldn't stop herself from flushing beneath his quizzical regard. He might find Julie's innocent comment amusing, she thought testily, but she certainly did not. Oh, it was all right for him. Unlike her he was quite at ease and experienced in these matters, whilst she . . .

'Come on.'

To her astonishment Vicky realised that Jay was heading for the front door. He saw her expression and smiled at her again.

'We might not be able to get back to the vicarage, but here we are in the town—we can go out and buy some nightclothes,' he explained with wry patience when she still looked bewildered 'and anything else we might need.'

He was of course quite right. Although, because of the one-way system, it had taken them some time to reach the house, on foot she knew it would only take them a matter of minutes to get back to the town centre.

What he said made sense and yet Vicky was aware of a reluctance to go with him—or to do anything that might increase the intimacy between them.

'We might as well get some food whilst we're about it,' Jay commented as they stepped outside.

The ground underfoot was treacherous and as he turned to lock the door behind them he slipped slightly. Acting automatically Vicky grabbed his arm as instinctively as she might have done one of the children. She could feel his muscles flex beneath her fingers; the sensation intensely disturbing. So much so that she released him quickly, as though the brief contact had burned her.

'Thanks.'

The cursory way in which he said it made her feel more uncomfortable, as though he, too, had been aware of her body's reaction to her touching him.

They walked to the shops in silence, Jay pausing outside the toy shop for a second whilst Vicky frowned.

She saw that he was looking at a BMX bike.

'Is this what Jamie wants?'

'Yes.' She sighed faintly. 'But it's out of the question this year. I simply can't afford it. He's saving towards it himself and I'm hoping there'll be enough by Christmas next year.'

Next door to the toy shop was a lingerie boutique, its window temptingly dressed with a selection of pastel silks and satins.

When Jay took her arm and turned towards the door Vicky tensed. 'Your nightdress,' he explained, frowning at her.

'Not from here.' Colour stung her face. 'It would be far too expensive. There's a chain store just down the road.'

To her fury Jay ignored her objections and pushed open the door of the shop. It was either go with him or cause a scene, Vicky decided, realising that they were attracting the attention of the girl standing behind the small counter.

Once inside, she felt embarrassment mingle with her anger. Just by being there Jay affected her.

'I . . .'

'We'd like a nightdress,' Jay interrupted, infuriating her with his cool assumption of control.

'Yes, of course.' The salesgirl smiled appreciatively at him, but then very few women would not, Vicky reflected sourly watching her. 'Is it a Chrismas present or——'

'Not exactly.'

'Did you have something specific in mind?'

Now she turned her attention to Vicky, but just as she was about to open her mouth again Jay forstalled her.

'The peach silk set in the window.'

Filled with dismay Vicky swallowed. She had glimpsed the silk nightdress with its matching twenties style short jacket as they walked past the window, but just a glimpse had been enough to convince her that it was way out of her price range; a fear which the salesgirl's complacent smile did nothing to subdue.

When she retreated to the rear of the shop Vicky hissed angrily to Jay. 'What on earth do you think you're doing? I could no more afford anything like that than I could fly. Besides it's a complete waste of money, I never wear anything like that.'

'No?' She didn't care for the derisive way Jay was smiling at her. 'Then perhaps it's time you did.'

Before she could make any further comment the salesgirl was back, carrying a cardboard box.

'That particular set is gift boxed,' she explained as she opened it. 'It's a rather special line we're stocking just for Christmas. Here we are.'

As she unfolded the nightdress from its bed of

tissue paper, Vicky could not quite hold back a tiny gasp of delight. Cut cleverly on the bias the bodice of the nightdress was supported by tiny shoestring straps which crossed at the back. The back of the nightdress was cut extremely low, and it crossed Vicky's mind as she fingered the delicate fabric that it could have been designed to be worn as an evening dress—or for a woman to wear for the pleasure of her lover . . . Unbidden the thought slipped into her mind and she released the fabric instantly, her body suddenly hot and uncomfortable.

'And this is the jacket that goes with it.'

Plainly the salesgirl was unaware of her discomfort. She held up the jacket for their inspection. Of an unusual design the hem was longer at the back than the front. The fabric again cut on the bias so that it fell gracefully in elegant folds, its plainness offset by the beautifully worked lace butterflies that trimmed its edges. In fact the lace was so delicate that Vicky was reluctant to touch it.

Of course it was far, far beyond her reach. Even if she had the money to buy it she would not have done so. There were far too many other things that were more important. It was ridiculous of Jay to have insisted that they come in here. She was just shaking her head regretfully when she realised the salesgirl was not looking at her, but at Jay, and moreover that she was beaming delightedly.

'We only ordered one set in each size,' she was telling him, adding to Vicky, 'Quite frankly I rather envy you . . . it's just the sort of thing I'd like for myself.'

Vicky whirled round, opening her mouth to protest, but the pressure of Jay's fingers on her arm stopped her. She could hardly make a scene in front of the salesgirl. But if Jay thought she was going to let him buy her ... Another, even more unwelcome thought struck her. Perhaps it wasn't for her, perhaps he had bought it for someone else. After all ...

'Now, something to eat I think,' Jay announced when they were back out on the street. 'Does this place have a decent delicatessen?'

It did—a small, exclusive shop that was far too expensive for Vicky to patronise, but she knew where it was. On the way they passed a chemists, and once again she found Jay taking control as he bundled her inside, and bought toothbrushes and other small necessities.

Outside again, it was still snowing and she was beginning to get very cold despite all her protective clothing. Jay must be frozen she reflected, glancing at him, but when he touched her arm, drawing her attention to a men's clothing shop, his ungloved fingers felt quite warm.

They both went inside and ten minutes later waiting for him whilst he payed for the towelling robe he had bought, she wondered how he would have reacted if she had insisted on paying for it. Rather grimly she decided that it might have been worth depleting her bank account just for the pleasure of finding out.

'Right, food, and then back to the house before the weather deteriorates any further.'

Already the cold afternoon was drifting into dusk. The snowflakes still fell, and Vicky did not think it was merely her imagination that told her the temperature was dropping, the wind icier than ever.

Inside the delicatessen Jay once again took charge, although she had to admit he was scrupulous about asking her what she liked. In a way it was very pleasant to be taken care of in such a way, although of course shopping was far, far easier when a budget didn't have to be taken into account, she reflected bitterly, unable to stop her mouth from watering as Jay bought delicious looking smoked salmon; crusty wholemeal bread, creamy butter, a rich paté, and then some cheese.

He had spent as much on those few delicacies as she allowed herself for a month's necessities, was the thought uppermost in her head as they left the shop.

'Hang on a sec.'

She stood helplessly on the pavement as Jay strolled into a small wine brokers. When he came out he was carrying yet another carrier bag. Vicky was so used herself to being burdened with bags full of shopping that she automatically reached for some of his, but he shook his head. 'No. It's okay, I can manage,' he assured her, adding with a grin, 'Just as long as you promise to catch me if I fall.'

Walking with him down the busy street, Vicky wondered how many men of his stature and wealth would be willing to be seen in such a domesticated role. In her experience men were more than willing to leave the boring chores of running a home to their wives, and that included the shopping. Henry, for instance, would never have dreamt of carrying plastic shopping bags. She shivered suddenly and her reaction had nothing to do with the cold. She didn't want to find things to admire in Jay, and it was then that she admitted to herself that she was fighting a desperate rearguard action against both him and herself. She knew quite well that physically he desired her; just as she knew that she desired him.

Looking at it objectively there was nothing wrong at all in both of them indulging that desire—it would offend or hurt no one. Morally it was far less 'wrong', if that was the word, than many other things she could think of. And yet she was frightened. What of, she asked herself? And numbingly she knew the answer. Of caring for him . . . of needing and wanting him. Ridiculous. She dismissed the fear abruptly, she was in no danger of doing anything of the sort.

'Time to head back I think.' Jay was looking at the overcast, dusky sky as he spoke, hurrying her through the crowded streets.

It was snowing in earnest when they reached the house, the footprints from when they came out, already covered with a fresh fall of snow.

'Key's in my pocket,' Jay told her, juggling his parcels on the top step. 'Can you get it for me?'

It was a simple enough request, but her stomach muscles contracted alarmingly as she slid her hand into the pocket of his jeans. Beneath the fabric she could feel the taut line of his hip. Her mouth had gone dry, and she desperately wanted to withdraw from him. Reminding herself that he would think her an absolute fool if he knew how just this casual contact with his body was disturbing her, she summoned all her will-power and forced herself to blot out the thoughts rioting through her mind—images of him naked, and her fingers touching his skin without the barrier of any fabric.

'Got it?'

Thankfully she had, and she hoped and prayed he would put the trembling of her fingers as she finally inserted the key into the lock down to the cold and nothing else.

Apparently he had because once they were inside he told her. 'Why don't you go upstairs and see if there's an immersion heater? A hot bath will soon drive away those shivers. If not we'll just have to hope that the central heating is better at heating the water than it is at heating the house. I'll go and see if I can get a fire started.

There was an immersion heater and Vicky switched it on before exploring the upper floor. The house had two bedrooms; both with double beds, both attractively furnished in pretty Laura Ashley fabrics and wallpaper. The bathroom was decorated in fresh olive tones and white, the airing cupboard thankfully still stocked with towels.

'Lucky for us that the people who lived here aren't moving out until they come back from holiday. They have a daughter in the States, and this Christmas visit to see her has been planned for a long time. The manager of the factory, to whom this house was rented, has to vacate it under the terms of the sale.'

'I thought you said it was bought for the son.'

'Yes, originally, but then it was let to the factory manager on a peppercorn rent.'

'So he's not just losing his job but his house as well.' Vicky remembered how, the first time she had seen him, she had been struck by a certain hardness about Jay. She shivered involuntarily.

'Is that how you see me?' His voice was distinctly unamused. 'You're quite wrong. In fact I wanted him to stay on. He's extremely good at his job, but he wants to take early retirement. He and his wife are thinking of moving to America to be with their daughter, and because of the job situation over there he can only go as a retired man. Also, because he's a sensible man, he's been putting the money he saved by having cheap accommodation on one side, and with the early retirement lump sum he gets, he'll be quite comfortably off.'

Chagrin stroked guilty colour over her high cheekbones as Vicky turned away from him. Suddenly, the confines of the small landing seemed unbearably narrow. To get past Jay to come downstairs she would practically have to touch him. She shuddered deeply, not knowing whether it was with fear or desire.

'Which bedroom do you want?' she managed to ask him, swallowing painfully as she saw the way he was looking at her.

'Which do you want?'

Again colour stained her skin. What would he say if she told him 'Yours?'

'I don't mind.'

'Well then, have this one.' It was the door nearest to them and he walked into it, dropping the cardboard box from the lingerie boutique on to the bed. He didn't, Vicky noticed, say anything to her about the other bedroom.

'I can't wear that,' she told him huskily, avoiding looking at him. 'It's far too expensive. I simply can't afford it.'

'No one's asking you to ... it's a gift.' His mouth compressed as he looked into her eyes. 'Don't be so damned proud and stubborn,' he told her softly, 'I've managed to get a fire lit. What do you want to do about eating?'

'Can you wait until I've had a bath?'

'No problem. Fancy a cup of coffee in the meantime?'

'Yes, I'll come down and make it.'

'No need. I'll do it. The Ellisons left their

cupboards fairly well stocked and I'm sure they won't mind us making use of them. I've located some beans and a grinder.'

It was an unusual sensation for Vicky to be able to just sit down and relax. Normally there were so many tasks for her to do that she wasn't used to having idle hands. On impulse she decided to ring home again, but to her dismay the line was dead.

It wasn't unknown for this to happen during the winter, but it worried her sufficiently for Jay to demand when he walked in with her coffee, 'What's wrong?'

'I tried to ring home, but the line's gone dead.'

'Stop worrying, the kids know where you are, and they're sensible enough for all their high spirits. You've done a good job with them.' His quiet words of praise stunned her. 'And you're an expert of course,' she mocked to cover her confusion. The anger that blazed in his eyes stunned her.

'You could say that,' he agreed tersely. 'Or at least more to the point, I'm an expert on how not to bring them up.'

What did he mean? Did he have children somewhere after all?

'Nothing like that.' He was becoming far too expert at probing her thoughts. 'I don't have any of my own. If I did, you can be damn sure they'd be brought up very differently than I was. Oh, I don't mean showered with material things,' he checked her. 'I'm talking about love and attention . . . two parents united in their desire to give their children a secure background.

'I was brought up by my aunt and uncle—I was illegitimate. I was a responsibility neither of them wanted. You couldn't have wanted the twins when you first discovered you were pregnant.'

She couldn't deny it, even whilst her heart ached for him after what he had just revealed to her. 'Abortion wasn't legal then,' she told him, adding honestly, 'if it had been I don't know what I would have done. I had only just started at university.'

'Why weren't you on the pill?'

She looked at him blankly. What on earth could she say? Fortunately, he didn't seem to want a response. 'You obviously love them.' He was talking about the twins again and now she felt she was on safer ground.

'Very much,' she agreed, 'even though they drive me mad at times. They both have so much energy. In fact I tend to worry more about Charles than I do about them. He's very conscious of his responsibilities ... he worries a good deal.'

'Had he no relatives he could have gone to when your husband died?'

The cruelty of his remark cut through her. 'I wouldn't have let them take him.' Her eyes flashed indignation. 'Poor baby ... his mother died when he was born, and Henry was a loving but remote father, and he was only five when Henry died. He was just beginning to come out of his shell a bit. I couldn't have let anyone else take him. Besides,' she looked at him squarely, 'one of the reasons Henry married me was because of Charles. He knew he was very ill and going to die. We talked the whole thing through before we married ... neither of us knew then that he would die so soon ... He thought he would be leaving us well cared for financially but his investments turned out to be bad ones.' Her chin lifted as he looked at her in silence. 'I know you're probably thinking I married him for security and money, but I didn't. I was at my wits end, only eighteen, pregnant. I knew by then I wanted to keep my baby . . . Henry knew all the circumstances, we had something to give each other . . .'

'But you were never lovers?'

He asked the question quietly, so quietly that she never thought to lie.

'Never,' she admitted. 'Even if . . . he wasn't well enough . . . I . . .'

'And since then?'

Now he was questioning her too personally. She had no desire for her sexual inexperience to be revealed for his scrutiny. 'That's hardly any of your business.' She drank her coffee, put down the cup and stood up. 'I'll go and have my bath, the water should be hot by now.' On her way to the door she paused and said angrily, 'I haven't asked you about your sex life.'

His eyes met hers, glinting suddenly. 'Ask,' he told her softly. 'What would you like to know?'

Why was it he always managed to get the better of her? She swore under her breath as she stubbed her toe on the top stair. Damn the man, he was getting under her skin, affecting her in ways that her mind and body both told her were dangerous.

She went into the bathroom and ran a bath whilst stripping off her clothes. Her jeans were soaked from the snow, and clung clammily to her legs.

She hadn't realised how cold she was until she sank into the deliciously warm water. Just to lie there without being interrupted by half-a-dozen requests for school books or food was a luxury in itself. Closing her eyes she let herself drift, coming to abruptly when she realised the direction her thoughts were taking. Her face flamed. What was the matter with her? Was she obsessed by the thought of Jay Brentford's body?

If you don't know what's the matter with you by now my girl, then something *is* wrong with you, she told herself as she stepped out of the bath and briskly towelled herself dry.

The thought of putting her damp jeans back on was distinctly off-putting. Maybe she could borrow something from her absent hostess, she reflected, wrapping a large towel round herself and picking up her clothes and heading for her bedroom.

Rather hesitantly she opened a wardrobe, letting out a relieved sigh as she saw it contained women's clothes. All she needed was a skirt, she could wear her own shirt. She found a plain dark brown one, which although too large for her was better than her wet jeans. As she put it on the bed she caught sight of the parcel on the bed. Unwillingly she was drawn to it, her fingers trembling slightly as she opened the box and took the nightdress out of its tissue wrapping. The fine silk slithered through her fingers. Unwrapping her towel, Vicky pulled it over her head, shivering deliciously as the fabric rippled sensually over her skin.

It fitted her perfectly, the delicate peach colour emphasing the creamy delicacy of her skin, making the red gold colour of her hair so much more startling. She had never worn anything as luxurious in her life, nor anything as sexy, she amended, staring at her own reflection in the mirror. The silk caressed the feminine thrust of her breasts, and clung wickedly to her hips. She moved and the nightdress moved with her, fluid as water, clinging to her legs. She turned and glanced at the back view, suppressing a faintly shocked gasp. It was cut so low at the back that it was practically indecent, and would crease like mad if she slept in it, she told herself. But then this nightdress had never been designed to be slept in.

Telling herself rather grimly that she was foolish even to try it on, she was just about to take it off when her bedroom door opened and Jay walked in. For a moment neither of them moved or spoke, and then Jay said softly, 'It suits you.'

'No. I . . .' Vicky was startled by the panic washing through her denial.

'You what?' His mouth was grim. 'You hate looking like a desirable woman? Do you think I don't *know* that? But you are,' he told her silkily as his hands closed on her shoulders. 'So extremely desirable that I find it impossible to resist you.' His mouth touched the side of her neck, and even though she knew she should be pulling away, Vicky found herself melting beneath his touch.

The delicate movement of his lips feathering tiny kisses along her skin made her shiver in pleasure, his tongue touched the frantic pulse beating in her throat and she groaned, clutching his jumper. Beneath the fine silk her heart was jumping like a steam engine. She heard him say her name and looked at him with eyes glazed with a mixture of shock and desire. 'Kiss me.'

She opened her mouth to refuse and then stopped. What was happening to her? She no longer seemed to be in control of her own reactions. As though it were no longer a part of her, she watched her hand lift to touch his face. His jaw was rough with an afternoon's growth of beard, she could feel it rasping beneath her fingertips. She knew that he was watching her, but

it seemed unimportant, outside the strange
weakness that seemed to possess her. Her fingertip
touched the corner of his mouth and traced the
outline of his lips uncertainly. She felt his fingers
curl round her wrist, imprisoning it. His lips
parted, his tongue touching her fingers, caressing
them as he slowly sucked on them.

Sensation sheeted through her, convulsing her
body, shocking her out of her dream world. How
could such a delicate caress be so arousing?

'Jay?' The sound of his name was lost against
his mouth as he kissed her. His mouth on hers was
gentle and yet it conveyed a passion which made
her shake in mute response. His tongue parted her
lips and her eyes flickered open to meet his.
Passion, dark and overriding, stared back at her
from his eyes, reaction kicking at her stomach, her
mind reeling away from her own passionate
response to him. Somehow they were on the bed
and she was helping him to remove his sweater . . .
then his shirt. His skin felt smooth beneath her
fingertips; smooth and hot. She wasn't sure which
one of them it was who groaned as her hands
moved exploratively on his skin. He kissed her
slowly, framing her face with his hands, his mouth
savouring the taste and texture of hers, his tongue
stroking delicately over her lips until she clutched
at him in mute protest, meeting the fierce surge of
desire she could feel within him with a feverish
response of her own.

This was what she had ached for from the
moment she set eyes on him she admitted to
herself as his mouth caressed her throat and then
moved down over her skin, down to the barrier of
her silk nightdress and over it, seeking almost
blindly. Her body tensed, her muscles contracted

savagely as his lips found her nipple, caressing it
through the fine silk, making her twist and arch
against him in a passionate frenzy, ready to tear
the delicate fabric from her body herself to destroy
the barrier between them.

When he released her, lifting his body away
from her, sheer savage disappointment shuddered
through her. She opened her eyes in mute protest
and discovered that he was merely removing the
remainder of his clothing.

She watched him, her heart thudding, touching
her tongue to her dry lips when he stepped out of
his trousers. If anything she had underestimated
the masculinity of him. Her mouth felt dry, her
body a tight, coiling ache that went on and on.

'My God, will you stop doing that.'

The tortured savagery of his words drew her
eyes to his face. Hectic colour lay along his cheek-
bones, his eyes were almost black, glittering
feverishly, his eyes on her mouth as she touched it
with her tongue again in nervous reaction.

'If you want to do that, then do it to me,' he
muttered thickly, reaching for her and pulling her
into his arms so that her head lay against his chest.
The musky, male scent of him aroused her
unbearably. She kissed him, feeling the heat
coming off his skin, feeling his muscles clench
beneath the soft caress of her mouth. His hand
found her breast and caressed it urgently, his
mouth exploring the satin softness of her skin. The
need she had felt earlier was nothing compared to
the tight, coiling ache she was experiencing now.
Her teeth nipped protestingly at his skin, resenting
the barrier of fine silk that still lay between them,
her muscles responding eagerly and fluidly to him
when he tugged it off.

Despite the twins' birth her body was un-blemished, her skin firm over her muscles, and she stretched sensually like a small cat beneath the caress of his eyes, shuddering in delicious pleasure as he bent to take the thrusting tip of one breast between strong teeth, tugging softly.

Unaware of what she was doing she raked her fingers down his back, trying so suppress the moan of pleasure that rose to her lips as she arched eagerly into him. She had no experience to guide her, only instinct; and it was instinct that told her that her eager responsiveness had shredded his self-control. She felt his abandonment of it, in the fierce possession of her breasts by his mouth and gloried in her responsiveness to it.

How could this be her? Vicky wondered in dazed bemusement. It was impossible to equate the way she was behaving with the cool disinterest she had previously felt in sexual fulfilment. Right now there was nothing more important to her than that Jay continue to stroke and caress her ... nothing she desired more than to reach the culmination her senses told her his body promised.

'Dear God, but I want you.' He muttered the words against her skin, as helpless beneath the onslaught of primaeval desire as she was herself, and like her he too, she suspected, was caught off guard by it.

As his hand stroked over her body and came to rest at the juncture of her thighs, gently cupping and then slowly exploring the femininity of her, her lack of experience and fear that he would reject her for it was forgotten, the wild, clamorous turmoil he aroused in her blood obliterating everything except the sheer need to respond; a sensation so primitive and compelling that Vicky doubted if she could have resisted it even if she had wanted to.

The sensation invoked by the caress of his fingers blasted apart all her previously held misconceptions, obliterating the one tiny part of her that had remained aloof, shocked by the intimacy of what he was doing. Instinctively Vicky arched wantonly against the pressure of his hand, her hands gripping his shoulders, her head falling back against the pressure of his mouth against her throat, and then her breasts, as spirals of pleasure started to build up inside her, triggering off delicate shudders of reaction. Heat seemed to envelop her body, her skin hot and tight, echoing the ache building up deep inside her. Her hips moved rhythmically, her body arching in a swift spasm of pleasure. All the breath seemed to leave her lungs all at once, and she fought desperately to release her mouth from Jay's, all pride and modesty abandoned in her aching need to tell him that his caresses had aroused her to the point of completion, but he wouldn't let her, savaging her mouth with the intensity of his kiss, the deft experienced touch of his fingers inciting her body to overthrow her restraint.

What followed was a minor revelation, the intensity and urgency of her response to him was so total that she was left in awe of her own sexuality. How could she have reached the age of twenty-seven without realising exactly what her body was capable of? Slowly, as the shudders of pleasure racking her body retreated, her mind started to function again. Jay had given to her a physical satisfaction she had never thought to know, but he had not actually possessed her. Why? She looked down the length of their bodies, her eyes widening slightly when she saw that his hand still cupped the red-gold triangle of hair between her thighs. Her glance slid from her body to his, instantly aware of his state of arousal. She swallowed tensely, burdened by a lack of experience.

'Aren't you going to thank me?'

Beneath the husky purr of his words she caught the masculine sexual arrogance and her throat tensed, the muscles locking. He had just been playing with her, she thought bitterly, just amusing himself at her expense. She struggled to move away from him, gasping her indignation as his hand spread possessively over her abdomen, the weight of his arm keeping her pinned to the bed. 'Well?' he demanded, adding mockingly, 'And don't tell me you didn't enjoy every minute of it . . .'

Desire had gone, to be replaced by seething resentment and humiliation. How dare he talk to her like that? She wanted to strike out at him and burst into tears at the same time. She felt almost light-headed and oddly weak. 'What do you want me to do,' she demanded bitterly, 'get down on my knees and kiss your . . .' She had been about to say 'feet', but the look in his eyes made her skin burn and her blood heat to boiling point. Unable to look away from him she could only try to fight down the wave of sensual awareness flooding through her body.

Putting his mouth against hers, he kissed her. Slowly at first and then with mounting passion, at the same time arching her into his body until her every pulse beat echoed its fierce throb. When he released her mouth she was dizzy, overwhelmed by the return of desire within herself, unable to comprehend how she could ache so, when not ten minutes before . . . Bewildered by the savage intensity of the desire she could sense seething within him she said huskily, 'I thought you mustn't want me . . .'

In the dimness of the unlit room she saw the white glimmer of his teeth as he smiled. 'Allow me to tell you that for a woman of twenty-seven you are unbelievably naïve.'

Instantly she recoiled and would have pulled away from him, but he wouldn't let her. 'Of course I want you my innocent little idiot,' he muttered thickly against her throat, 'but your need of *me* wouldn't wait and being the gentleman that I am . . .' Beneath the soft drawl, Vicky thought she could sense amusement and it goaded her into tensing and arching her body in a vain effort to dislodge him. As she lay beneath him tremors of helpless rage shook her body. She felt him move and thought he meant to release her until she heard him mutter something savagely beneath his breath and then he was between her thighs touching her, not gently this time, but in a way that brought a fierce surge of pleasure to her body, so that almost without knowing it she was arching against him, demanding and receiving the fierce thrust of his body within her own.

As he moved within her, possessing her, his mouth found her breasts, tormenting the already swollen peaks until she felt that she might die from the aching agony he was inflicting on her.

Of their own accord her legs wrapped round his, her hips lifting, moving rhythmically to the urgent thrust of his body. Sweat broke out on his skin, and she tasted the moisture with her tongue as he lifted his head from her breasts, the muscles of his throat ridged and powerful as he thrust fiercely within her.

Wave after wave of tumultuous release shuddered through her, her muscles contracting tightly round him, drawing from him a savage cry of fulfilment. Still trembling in the aftermath of their mutual climax, Vicky was surprised to hear herself asking huskily, 'Isn't it now your turn to thank *me*?'

She heard him laugh, as he buried his mouth in her throat, licking the fine sheen of sweat from her skin. As he rolled over and pulled her against his side, she heard him saying wickedly. 'Not for *that* my dear—after all it was mutually pleasurable, but should you ever be able to shed your inhibitions sufficiently to kiss . . .' He laughed again as she covered her ears, outraged by what she suspected he was about to say.

'Was he your first lover . . . the twins' father?' The abrupt and unexpected question coming so closely after his teasing caught her off guard.

Chagrined because he was so obviously aware of her naïveté and inexperience, she said bitterly, 'I'm sorry that my experience doesn't match your own . . .'

'I'm not.' The sudden intensity in his voice silenced her. He reached across her, snapping on a bedside lamp. His hair was tousled, his skin gleaming in the soft light. A faint tug of desire shivered through her, shocking her. What was it about this man that made her want him so?

'Why did you let me make love to you?'

Avoiding his eyes Vicky countered wryly, 'Could I have stopped you?'

His fingers touched her jaw, making her turn back to face him. 'If you had really wanted to, yes. I don't go in for rape.' His voice was suddenly implacable and cold. 'It's obviously been a long time since you've had a lover.' His eyes narrowed on her face and he said softly, 'At a guess I'd say an extremely long time. So I repeat, why me?'

Somehow she managed a nonchalant shrug. Was he already regretting making love to her; thinking that because of her inexperience she was going to demand more from him than he was prepared to give? Her skin burned ... 'Surely I don't need to tell you that you're an extremely attractive man. My life is such that it's very rare for me to meet a man like you. Who can say why they feel desire for a specific person. Why did you want me?'

His mouth compressed. 'You're trying to avoid the question.'

Turning away from him she said huskily. 'I wanted to be made love to ... is that so hard to understand? The only men I get to meet are normally the husbands of friends.' She shrugged again. 'Widows in my position have to be very careful. I don't want to become embroiled in an affair with someone else's husband. You have no ties ... or at least none that I'm aware of. Physically you're very attractive ...'

'And that's all it was? Merely the need to fulfil a sexual urge?'

'What else could it be?'

For some reason the look in his eyes made her feel uncomfortable; as though he had caught her out in a lie, but she wasn't lying ... That was all she had wanted, even though it did sound almost sordid, worded the way he had worded it. What on earth had he expected her to say? That she had fallen madly in love with him? Ridiculous. And yet as she watched him move off the bed and pick up his discarded clothes she was filled with a tiny ache that had nothing to do with physical dissatisfaction. Men were always using women for purely physical completion and thought none the worse of themselves or each other for it, so why should he be making her feel so ... so ... so guilty, she fumed, dressing quickly once he had gone. She had no reason whatsoever to feel guilty, none at all.

# CHAPTER SEVEN

VICKY had expected there to be a degree of constraint between them after what had happened and had deliberately held back from going downstairs for as long as she could, but eventually the hunger pangs tearing at her stomach refused to let her stay.

She found him seated by the fire, glancing at a magazine, and paused awkwardly by the door, until eventually he looked up. There was nothing in his eyes to betray what he was feeling—if anything. Perhaps it hurt his pride to know that he had been wanted simply as a sex object, she thought with relish, if so, it would do him good to suffer a little of what her sex suffered all the time. A little surprised by her own thoughts she said hurriedly, 'I'm starving . . . what about something to eat?'

'Good idea,' he agreed, putting his magazine down and standing up, smiling at her as calmly as though there had never been the slightest degree of intimacy between them. Beneath her checked blouse Vicky could feel her heart thumping heavily as he came towards her. What on earth was wrong with her, she wondered crossly; she was reacting to his proximity now even more intensely than she had done before they had been lovers. It was ridiculously irrational.

'If you want a hand . . .'

'I can manage.' She knew she sounded rather desperate, and her pulses were already thudding at

the thought of having to work in the close confines
of the small kitchen with him there as well.

With all the delicacies he had bought it was no
problem to create an appetising supper and
placing everything on a trolley she had found
Vicky wheeled it into the small sitting room. Jay
had built up the fire whilst she had been at work in
the kitchen, the heat it gave off relaxing her
numbed muscles. As she walked in Jay rose to
meet her, taking the trolley off her and positioning
it between two fireside chairs. 'Good idea,' he
approved, studying it. 'There is a small dining
room, but in view of the inadequate heating we
will be far warmer eating in here.' He glanced at
the trolley and frowned, 'Just a minute.'

What had she forgotten? Vicky wondered,
watching him disappear in the direction of the
kitchen. He was back within seconds, carrying a
bottle of champagne and two glasses.

All the time they were eating her thoughts were
not on the food but on what had happened
upstairs. Logic and feeling had never seemed so
very far apart. Even now she was having to stop
herself from reaching out and touching him. She
shivered slightly, glad of the trolley between them,
stunned into shocked stillness when Jay drawled
blandly, 'Did you enjoy it?'

At first she thought he had actually read her
thoughts and knew that her mind had been on
their lovemaking and her own overwhelming
response to it, and colour flared delicately along
her cheek-bones. His expression changed, something faintly alarming glinting in his eyes as he
added softly, 'I meant the food, but you *are* quite
right, there are other appetites that it is far more
enjoyable to satisfy than the hunger for food.' He

picked up a champagne glass and handed it to her.

'You know you intrigue me,' he said slowly. 'You're like no other woman I've ever met.'

Vicky grimaced faintly, she could well imagine how different she was from his normal female friends.

'You mean a case of any port in a storm,' she offered hardily, sipping the bubbling liquid, and trying to subdue the ache in her heart. This was the first time she had actually drunk champagne, she realised with a start. Her wedding had been a quiet one, with no celebrations afterwards, and there had been no other occasions in her life to merit buying it—not just for herself.

'Is that how you see yourself?' He was frowning, she realised, reminding her of the *hauteur* she had sensed in him at their first meeting.

'Well, I can hardly compare in quality of looks to the sort of women you normally . . . make love to.'

'You don't think so?' His smile was thin. 'Certainly they possess a good deal more gloss and they're very attractively and expensively packaged.'

His voice was so derisory that she could not resist asking. 'If you despise them so much then why . . .?'

'Why take them to bed? Do you really need to ask me that?' he said silkily. 'I should have thought it was self-evident. A man is in no danger of becoming over-involved with a glossy, mechanical doll.'

Suddenly her heart was thumping madly, her body tense with a mingling of expectancy and dread. She was shaking so much she had to put her champagne glass down.

'With you it's different,' Jay told her quietly.

'You're a real woman with a mind that's as healthily attractive as your body.'

'What are you trying to say to me?' Her voice was strained and husky. Please God don't let her misunderstand him and place too much importance on his words. If she did and was then proved wrong how could she bear the pain of knowing . . . Inexorably her thoughts slid on despite all her attempts to halt them. It was useless now to protest to herself that his attraction for her was purely physical. It wasn't and it never had been. She started to tremble wildly, and heard his voice above the pounding thud of her heart.

'I don't really know. Perhaps that I'm drawn to you in a way that I just can't rationalise, that I want more from you than the mere physical release of losing myself in your body. That, illogical or not, when you smile at me the whole day brightens . . .' He grimaced wryly and added in a completely emotionless voice, 'I suspect what I'm trying to tell you is that against all logic and everything else I've ever believed in the way I feel about you comes dangerously close to that much-suspect emotion "love".'

Love! He loved her? Vicky felt herself floundering desperately torn between joy and disbelief.

'But we hardly know one another.' It sounded so ridiculous that she couldn't quite repress a small giggle. The wry slant of Jay's eyebrows informed her that he shared her feelings.

'It does seem unlikely, I agree. Love *per se* is not an emotion I have too much faith in. Once, many years ago, I believed myself in love and I thought that feeling was returned—until my fiancée broke off our engagement to marry a man twenty years older than me and twenty times richer . . .

So that explained the hard reticence she had sensed in him, Vicky reflected, watching him as the logs cast shadows over his face. There had been little that was loverlike in his remarks to her and yet strangely she felt them to be more believable and genuine for that lack.

'This afternoon shopping with you . . . somehow it felt so right. Just the same way that living with you and the kids does.'

His words caused her a certain degree of disquiet. 'Maybe the attraction is simply that of a different way of life,' she suggested neutrally.

'You mean overworked tycoon falls for the back-to-nature myth?' He shook his head. 'No, I don't think so.' He smiled at her then. 'I suppose you're wondering why I'm telling you all this?'

'No woman ever wonders why a man tells her he thinks he might be in love with her.'

'Not so much in love, but able to love,' Jay corrected. 'I feel able to love you.' He looked at her with narrowed eyes. 'What I'm asking is do you feel the same way sufficiently for us to try and see if we do have something mutually strong enough to build a future on?'

'A future?' She moistened her lips nervously. 'You mean with me as your mistress . . . and you visiting me?'

He shook his head firmly before she could go any further. 'No, that's not what I mean. I mean a future that includes the kids, a wedding ring and words like forever.'

For the first time the logical way he was talking to her chilled her a little, but how could she blame him for that? Being logical was one of his strongest traits, and if she was honest with herself could she have believed him had he told her he was head

over heels in love with her? He was thirty-odd,
experienced and worldly and she was so deeply
attracted to him that right from the start she had
been appalled by her own feelings. Could they call
their feelings love? She had nothing to compare
her own feelings with. Apart from the odd teenage
crush she had never experienced the complexities
of love. With the twins and Charles to bring up
there had simply never been time. She had tried to
explain away the way she felt about him as purely
physical desire, but she knew she had not been
honest with herself. There was more to it than
that.

'All I'm suggesting is that we give one another
time to discover how strong our feelings are. An
old-fashioned period of courtship if you like.'

'With access to my bed thrown in.'

Holding her eyes he said levelly, 'A good sexual
relationship helps to build a good marriage. If we
didn't take pleasure in one another sexually I
wouldn't be talking to you like this now. But I
don't want you simply for sex.'

No, he wouldn't, Vicky reflected. A man like
Jay would never have to look hard for someone
to share his bed.

'Is that why you . . . you made love to me this
afternoon? A sort of test?'

She was being unfair and she knew it, seeing her
own judgment of herself reflected in his eyes.

'I made love to you this afternoon for one
reason and for one reason alone . . . and that was
simply that over these past days wanting you has
made my body ache so much that I simply
couldn't wait any longer. When we first talked,
you implied that the twins' father was merely one
among many lovers you had had. I suspect that

that was far from the truth.' He saw her open her mouth and continued firmly. 'What happened in the past is the past, and the only reason I'm bringing it up now is because I want you to know that no matter how many or how few men there have been in your past my feelings for you are for the woman you are today. We all make mistakes in life . . .' He looked so grave suddenly that Vicky wondered what he was thinking about. A dark, almost brooding look filled his eyes. Was he thinking about the girl he had loved and lost? The sharp stab of jealousy lancing through her made her ache.

'You throw up a defensive barricade around yourself to keep my sex at bay, which tells me that at some time you've been very badly hurt by someone or something.'

His words made her throat ache and Vicky longed to confide in him, but she just could not find her voice. If she did, might he not turn from her in disgust? A girl who gets so drunk at a party that she goes to bed with a stranger . . . a stranger she can't even visualise now . . . She shuddered and came out of the past to hear him saying quietly. 'Should we eventually decide to marry, I should like to legally adopt Charles and the twins. It will safeguard both us and the twins if at some future date their father should turn up. I've seen enough of what it can do to kids to be torn between two parents not to wish that upon any child.'

'You've got it all planned out.'

He smiled then. 'But it still all depends on you. We've made love now. You've satisfied your curiosity about me . . .' He saw her expression and smiled, 'Oh yes, I knew that you wanted me, but what I didn't know and still don't . . . is whether it was just curiosity?'

He was asking her a question, and it was one she would have to answer. 'I don't think so.'

Vicky was relieved when he didn't press her any further, simply topping up her champagne glass and saying softly, 'Then let's both drink a toast to the future—our future.'

After that, amazingly, the constraint she had felt before simply fell away and before too long they were chatting companionably. It was, indeed, almost as though she had known him for many years she thought in some amazement, listening whilst he made a dry comment about his early days in business.

'And you were at university in Bristol? I know the city quite well, I had friends who lived there.' He frowned, his eyes going dark and Vicky wondered if he was perhaps thinking of the girl he had loved again.

'You're all but going to sleep. Why don't you go up.'

'After I've cleared up,' Vicky told him glancing at the trolley.

'I'll do that,' Jay offered, getting up and stretching, flexing long bones and taut muscles. As she watched him a heat seemed to grow in her stomach, an ache that flooded her body with sharp desire. If nothing else, marriage to Jay would bring her a physical satisfaction she had never thought to know, she reflected as she made her way upstairs. It was stupid to feel disappointed because he had not kissed her good night, nor had he made any mention of joining her.

She heard him come upstairs just after she got into bed. He went into the other bedroom and then the bathroom. Lying tensely in her bed Vicky heard him returning to the other bedroom. Disappointment flooded her. She bit her bottom lip, angry with herself for feeling the way she did. Turning over she pulled the bedclothes over her head, trying to ignore the mental pictures forming in her brain, trying to blot out the image of Jay's body.

'Vicky.'

The sudden sound of her name, plus the sensation of the bed dipping, jolted her upright. Jay was seated on the bed, two glasses in his hand and a bottle of champagne in the other. He snapped on the bedside lamp and she watched his eyes darken.

'What happened to the nightdress?'

Until that moment she had forgotten she was completely nude. 'I didn't want to crease it.'

She heard him laugh and suddenly her body came alive. She didn't need champagne to make her feel light-headed she thought, watching him walk across the room and pluck the silk jacket from a chair. Coming back to her he draped it round her shoulders, the edges caressing the curves of her breasts.

'Here.' He poured the champagne and handed her a glass. The crystal chilled her fingers and the champagne spilled, splashing down on to her breasts as the jacket became dislodged in her attempt to steady her glass.

The laughter bubbling up in her throat died as she saw how Jay was looking at her. In a trance she watched as his dark head lowered to her breast, his tongue delicately lapping up the splashes of champagne.

A deep groan was wrenched from her throat,

her fingers locking in the crisp darkness of his
hair. Her breasts swelled to fill his palms, the
shuddering heat of his body against her, as he
pushed aside the duvet and wrenched off his robe,
excited her, her skin clinging moistly to his.

His lips and tongue stroked over her breasts,
teasing and playing with them until her nipples were
inflamed and tender, aching for the heat of his
mouth against them. She reached out blindly for him
sobbing his name in a ragged moan of need.

Holding her flat to the bed, he lifted his head,
his chest pumping savagely in time with his harsh
breathing. She could see his arousal and released
another husky moan, reaching out towards him,
embracing his body with her hands and then her
lips, glorying in the savage uncontrolled response
of his flesh to her caresses, hearing in the hoarse,
raw mutters of praise that rained feverishly on her
ears that he was as little able to control his need
for her as she was hers for him. Both of them were
perspiring, his back slick beneath her anxious
fingers as he arched over her. Her body ached to
be filled by his. She lifted her hips, grinding them
against his, grasping his body with her knees,
feeling the heady lack of control in him as he
groaned her name.

'I want . . . you, Vicky . . . I want you . . . Dear
God how much I want you.'

It was a litany chanted between harshly drawn
breaths, broken off only when her feverish fingers
slid down his back, investigating the taut planes of
his buttocks. She cried out as he entered her, not
with pain but with joy, eagerly opening her body
to his, willingly matching the savage intensity of
his lovemaking and glorying in her power to make
him cast aside the mantle of distant stranger and

become instead a man as much possessed by passion and need as she was herself.

In the peaceful lull that followed the explosive climax of their lovemaking she found herself turned into his arms and held there, her body warmed by his. She had never actually slept with anyone before, and she found the sensation extraordinarily moving, as much so in its own way as their previous physical union.

Towards dawn she woke, immediately conscious of his warmth beside her, and the arm he had flung across her body in sleep. For a long time she simply lay there, marvelling at his power to alter the axis of her world, and then she went over all that he had said to her the previous evening. Slowly, like the onset of a thaw, she could feel joy and hope rising up inside her. Suddenly the future looked bright and promising. He was not in love with her he had said but there could be love, surely more lasting and to be treasured than the mirage of mere adoring infatuation? She could love him too ... she could admit that now ... was indeed already half way to loving him. Content and more happy than she could ever remember being in her life before she closed her eyes and snuggled closer to him. In sleep his arm tightened protectively around her ... at least she thought it had been in sleep, until the lazy caress of his fingers against her breast made her realise that he was awake.

This time they made love slowly, almost tenderly, she reflected later, remembering how he had teased and aroused her skin with kisses until she was mindless with pleasure, the blood singing in her veins as they climbed together towards the human peak of perfection, and there was no reality apart from that which they created between them.

# CHAPTER EIGHT

As Jay had predicted the snow ploughs had been out during the morning, clearing the blocked roads. It was still bitterly cold but had stopped snowing and to Vicky's great relief when she rang home she discovered that the 'phone was once again working.

She spoke to all three children, as did Jay. Indeed, they seemed to have more to say to him than they did to her. Having assured herself that they were all still in one piece she replaced the receiver, and went to join Jay in the kitchen where he was busy making coffee.

After a leisurely breakfast they left the house just after eleven. She had never felt quite like this in her life before Vicky reflected seated beside him in his car. She felt him look at her and returned his look, blushing a little beneath it.

'Have I told you yet how infinitely desirable I find you, Mrs Moreton?' he asked quirking one eyebrow.

Vicky grinned at him. 'Not in so many words.'

'I hope it isn't going to take you long to make up your mind to marry me.'

When she looked at him he said wryly, 'I'm not much good at self-immolation. Sleeping in the same house, but not with you, is going to be murder, but the kids are sharp.'

'I thought both of us had some mind-making up to do,' Vicky reminded him.

He shook his head. 'Mine already is.'

'But you said . . .'

'I didn't want to panic you, but you seemed so receptive to the idea, that I've decided to come clean. I knew I wanted to marry you within hours of meeting you.' He laughed as he saw her expression. 'Don't ask me how, I don't know. All I do know is that initially it scared me sick. There I was one moment not a thought of marriage in my mind, the next minute, I'd seen you.' He shrugged lightly, leaving Vicky to cope with her amazement. 'Illogical I know, but unignorable.'

'After all you said to me yesterday,' Vicky protested heatedly.

'What could I say? That somehow the moment I saw you I knew I had to marry you?' He grimaced faintly. 'I was terrified you'd think I was mad, but what I said yesterday still stands. I'm not going to stampede you into anything if that's what you're frightened of.'

As they drove on to the main road the traffic became heavier and sitting in silence, to allow Jay to concentrate on his driving, Vicky became busy with her own thoughts. Jay was quite right in saying that they could hardly sneak in and out of one another's bedrooms with the children about. Charles in particular was at a sensitive age and she suspected it would make him feel extremely uncomfortable to know that they were lovers, as opposed to husband and wife. Children could be depressingly moral where their parents were concerned, she knew.

'I've got to go back to London for a couple of days just before Christmas,' Jay informed her. 'If you'll have me I'd like to spend Christmas itself with me and the kids—they need to get to know me better, but I don't want to wait too much into the New Year for you, Vicky.'

The New Year. Right now it seemed a long time away ... too long when she thought of all the nights in between when she would not be in his bed. And what did she really need to think about, an inner voice demanded uncautiously? She would never meet another man who aroused her as Jay did, especially a man whom she also liked and respected; whose company and conversation stimulated her mind as much as his touch did her body. The children liked him, and apart from Charles, had no other father to compare him with. On financial grounds alone many people would think she was a fool for even thinking of hesitation, but somehow money did not come into it. Swallowing nervously she said softly, 'Jay, I think I can give you your answer now ...' She protested as he braked suddenly, stopping the car, thankful that they had now turned off the main road and that they were alone. 'It's yes,' she told him, adding honestly, 'Everything's happened so quickly I don't know for sure exactly what I feel, except that I already know that I can't bear to think of my life without you.'

His voice thick, Jay responded. 'That's good enough for me.' The kiss they exchanged was mutually satisfying, broken only when another motorist drove past and sounded his horn.

In a bright-coloured daze Vicky sat beside Jay as he drove her home, still only half able to comprehend what she had committed herself to.

At Jay's insistence, once the excitement over their return had subsided, she took the children on one side and explained to them that Jay had asked her to marry him.

There was a brief silence, and then Charles asked her uncertainly. 'If you do will that mean that you'll leave us?'

That he should even think such a thing appalled her.

'Of course not! You're my family, Charles—all three of you, and if I do marry Jay he'll then become part of that family.' The relief on his face made her heart ache. Did he really think she would abandon him? Poor child, but then he'd already lost so much in his short life, no wonder he was so little inclined to trust and take things for granted in the way that the twins did.

There was no question of any of the children not liking Jay. Far from it, and she marvelled at the ease with which he communicated with them. For a man who by his own admission had had very little to do with children he seemed to have an instinctive way with them.

'I think you should marry him,' Charles said at last.

She looked at the twins. Both of them nodded their heads. 'Then we'll have a proper father,' Julie said determinedly.

'Will we still live here?'

That was Jamie, and his question stumped her. She and Jay had not talked about where they would live. He had his business interests to think about of course, and the house was really Charles'. She only held it in trust for him.

She put the question to Jay that evening after the children had gone to bed and they were alone. Already there was a rightness about having him there that frightened her. It was unnerving how quickly she had come to depend on his presence and how much she dreaded him not being there.

Was this then love? This need to have him beside her, to reach out and touch him as though to reassure herself that he was real, to go to sleep in his arms and wake up at his side ... She had an uneasy feeling that it must be.

'We can still live in this district if that's what you want,' he told her. 'There's no reason why I can't commute or even work at home, but what I would suggest is that we let this place and put the money on one side for Charles when he's older. Once we're married his education will be my responsibility so whatever small capital he already has can be left to grow until he comes of age. He'll need it if he's to maintain this place.

'You wouldn't want us to move to London then?'

'And deprive the kids of the freedom they have here?' He shook his head. 'No. It wouldn't be fair on them. They seem to have taken to the idea of our being married quite well.'

'Umm ... The twins are thrilled. Charles seems a bit reticent.'

'Because of his father?'

'Partially, and partially I think because he's worried that we might abandon him.'

She saw Jay frown as he put his arm round her and pulled her against his body. The old sofa sagged beneath their combined weight, and Vicky leaned her head on his shoulder, revelling in the warmth and security of him.

'Did he say that?'

'He hinted at it, but I've tried to reassure him. In many ways he's as much my child as the twins. After all he's never known any other mother, and simply because they are twins, somehow they're not quite as close to me as Charles is.'

'We'll find a way of allaying his fears, but now . . .'

His kiss made her ache for more than the frustrating clothed contact of their bodies, and instinctively she moved closer to him, pressing her body against his, moaning deep in her throat as his hand caressed her breast. He pushed aside her sweater, firelight dancing on the creamy globe of her breast. Desire shuddered through her and she arched wantonly against him.

'Stop tormenting me,' Jay muttered, pulling away from her. 'You know damn well we can't . . . and what you're doing to me.'

As he moved she saw the hard swell of his arousal and fought down an immediate impulse to reach out and touch him, but as though he had read her mind, he groaned and pulled her back down on the sofa, holding her, his hands biting into her skin. 'Vicky . . .' He broke off and swore, pushing her upright, and moving away from her, just in time she realised, as the sitting-room door opened and Jamie walked in.

'Jamie, you're supposed to be asleep,' she accused, amazed that Jay could have heard him coming when she had not, her mind deaf to everything but the inner cry of her need for him.

'I know, but I couldn't,' was his faintly belligerent reply. 'When you and Ma get married will you really be our father?' he asked Jay frowningly.

Vicky held her breath as Jay paused consideringly before replying. 'If that's what you want me to be, Jamie. No one's going to force you into making me something you don't want me to be. I should like you to consider me your father, but it must be your decision.'

Vicky allowed her breath to sigh slowly away as Jamie's frown cleared. 'Well, we do,' he told Jay firmly, 'but we thought you might want us to call you "uncle". That's what some of the others at school call their mother's boyfriends,' he added scornfully, 'but we don't like it.'

'Well that's probably because their parents are divorced,' Jay explained calmly, 'and those children already have a father, even if he doesn't live with them. Now, I think it's time you went back to bed, unless you've any more questions.'

Vicky watched as her son scowled ferociously.

'If you and Ma are getting married, does that mean that you'll be sleeping in her bed?'

Vicky sighed. Children were so sophisticated nowadays; there wasn't much they didn't pick up at school.

'Yes, but not until after we're married,' Jay responded evenly. 'Most married people do sleep together.' As he spoke he held Jamie's gaze unflinchingly. 'Will you mind?'

'No.' Jamie responded at last. 'I suppose it gets lonely for Ma sleeping all alone. Well, that's what Mrs Brady in the post office says. She says it's a lonely life for a woman on her own.'

'Bed,' Jay told him firmly, 'Come on I'll go with you.'

He was back within ten minutes.

'I wonder exactly how much they do know about adult relationships,' he murmured as he walked in. 'For one moment there your son was playing the extremely heavy parent.'

'I'm not sure if he realises the exact significance of "sleeping together",' Vicky told him.

'But he does seem to believe it's something to be disapproved of until sanctified by marriage,' he grimaced faintly. 'Thank God it's not long until the New Year.'

It was a comment that Vicky echoed many times over the next couple of weeks. Much as she enjoyed watching Jay establish a rapport with the children once school term had finished, she was tormented by the nagging ache of desire that never left her, and that had to be satisfied with brief, snatched, unfulfilling kisses, when her body ached for Jay's total possession.

She was in the kitchen making lunch, mentally ticking off all she had to do before Christmas, when her glance fell on her calendar, and she bit her lip suddenly remembering the Sterne's party. Should she cancel it? She thought about it and then rejected doing so. No, she would ring Philip and ask him if she might bring a friend.

Sensing his curiosity about her request, she was amused by his scrupulous avoidance of voicing it as he responded in the affirmative.

She told Jay about the invitation when he came in for lunch. 'Great, but what about the kids?'

All organised she told him, and as their eyes met she knew he was thinking not so much about the dinner party, but about the opportunity to be alone which it would give them.

The 'phone started to ring and as she went to answer it he murmured in her ear. 'Why don't we forget the party, and find somewhere where we can be alone instead?'

Shaking her head she picked up the receiver. 'It's for you,' she told him.

He had received a good many calls while he was staying with them, but this one seemed to take slightly longer to deal with.

'I've got to go to London for a meeting on

Christmas Eve,' he told her when he had finished. 'Damn.'

'But you'll be back for Christmas?'

Once she wouldn't have dreamed of allowing the anxiety in her voice to betray her, but now it didn't seem to matter if he heard how she felt.

'You can bet on that.'

'Don't forget we're going for the tree this afternoon,' Charles reminded him, interrupting them.

'Well, you can drop me off in town first,' Vicky decided. If she was going to take Jay to the Sterne's dinner party, then she was going to have a new dress for it. She was tired of him seeing her in jeans and jumpers; for once she wanted him to see her in something feminine.

An hour later they set out, the three children in the back of the car, Vicky sitting next to Jay in the front.

The snow still lay quite thickly on the ground, but the roads were now clear, although more snow had been forecast. Already people were saying it had been one of the worst winters on record, with more to come.

'Will here do you?' Jay asked, turning into the hotel car park. When she nodded he asked, 'What time do you want picking up?'

'About four?'

'Fine, that should give us enough time to get the tree and then we can all have a drink here before we go home.'

'Home'. How naturally he said the word, and how much pleasure it gave her to hear him say it. As she got out of the car he leaned across and kissed her briefly. Traitorously her lips wanted to cling to his, but conscious of the children watching them, Vicky disengaged herself.

She found the dress she wanted in a small boutique she knew about but never normally looked in—it sold good-quality designer clothes and was horrendously expensive, but surely for once she could afford to be extravagant?

It was a soft, slinky Monica Chong in matt black wool crêpe that did things to her skin and hair that even she found unbelievable. The owner of the boutique was frankly envious of her ability to get into the size eight, and looking at her reflection in the mirror Vicky knew it was a dress she had to have.

The decision made she found she needed shoes to go with it and on the boutique owner's advice tried a small shop tucked away down a narrow cobbled street. It was owned and run by a girl who designed and had made up her own shoes, and it didn't take long for Vicky to choose a pair of black satin shoes with high fragile heels, designed in such a way that they showed off her high instep and drew attention to the delicate bones of her ankles. Because she so seldom wore dresses or skirts, Vicky was unused to seeing her own unclad legs.

'You'll need silk stockings,' the girl in the shoe shop told her emphatically, 'or even better, if they've got any left, a pair of self-supporting ones that won't show under your dress. You can get some from Understudy, she added, mentioning the lingerie shop where Jay had bought her her nightdress.

It was three-thirty by the time she completed her purchases, having been tempted into some new make-up and a pair of frankly fake *diamanté* earrings with large fake pearl drops that she was assured were all the latest fashion.

By the time she reached the hotel car park, the others had already arrived. The largest, bushiest Christmas tree she could ever remember seeing was tied securely to the roof of Jay's car and as the children clambered out they started to tell her all about the trials and tribulations of acquiring it.

'What's in the bags?' Jamie demanded inquisitively, staring at her shopping.

'Nothing for you.' It wasn't quite true. On an impulse that she feared was fuelled as much by the guilt of what she had spent on herself as anything else, she had bought all three of them watches. The twins had been nagging for new ones for months and although she had spent more on them than she had intended, she already felt excited at the thought of seeing their faces when they unwrapped them. For Charles she had chosen a heavy-duty facsimile of a Rolex, knowing how grown up it would make him feel; for Jamie there was a digital watch with enough extra functions to keep him occupied at least for Christmas Day and for Julie a dainty gold-plated feminine wristwatch with a matching bracelet. The only person she hadn't bought anything for was Jay, she realised, watching him climb out of the car, but what could she buy for the man of his wealth? For some reason the thought depressed her.

'What's wrong?'

It amazed her how easily he read her emotions, and she admitted as they followed Charles and the twins into the hotel lounge. 'It just struck me that there's a huge difference in our financial status . . .' She wrinkled her nose and added, 'I suppose it sounds crazy but in many ways I wish you were less well-off . . . less . . .'

'I'm not expecting you to play the beggar-maid,

forever grateful and in awe, if that's what worries you,' he told her brusquely cutting across her words. 'Money might oil the wheels of life, but it doesn't turn them—emotion does that.'

Vicky found herself dwelling on his words as they sat down and were served a substantial afternoon tea. It was true that seen through her eyes Jay's life had been a bleak one, but he had chosen it. She was not naïve enough to believe that no other woman before her had wanted to share her life with him. So what did she have that they did not? But hadn't he already told her that?

'Umm ... that was great,' Julie sighed, sitting back replete and dragging Vicky's attention away from her thoughts. 'You know,' she commented looking at her mother with serious grey eyes, 'it makes me feel really good inside that you and Jay are getting married and he's going to be our father.' She blushed a bright red and lapsed into sudden silence, ignoring Jamie's brotherly, 'You're soppy!'

It was late that night before she got the children off to bed. After their evening meal had come all the excitement of putting up the tree. Jay had masterminded the whole thing, and looking at it now she had to admit they had done a first-class job. Sensing him standing behind her she said dreamily, 'Jay, if you don't mind I'd like to be married in church.'

'That's no problem, apart from the delay.'

She laughed and teased. 'What, you mean you aren't going to rush out and get a special licence?'

It was immensely reassuring to her that they had developed this teasing rapport between them. At times the intensity of her physical desire for him frightened her, and she needed this lighter side of their relationship to make her feel that she was still in touch with the person she had been before he came into her life. As she turned round he took her in his arms, his mouth feathering lightly across her own. As always she felt a swift surge of excitement inside her, her body melting, yielding to the hardness of his. His kiss hardened, becoming possessive and demanding. In a thick voice he muttered. 'Do you think there's one chance in hell that those impossibly energetic brats won't come downstairs tonight?'

His reference to the fact that every night since they had returned from their overnight stay in Camwater and had announced their intention to marry, they had at some point or another during the evening been interrupted by the arrival of one or other of the children made her sigh and smile.

'I sense they suspect that my ability to be the guardian of my own morals has been seriously undermined.'

'How seriously?' His hand was already sliding down her body, triggering off frantic pulses. There was nothing . . . nothing on this earth she wanted more than for Jay to make love to her. Right now . . . right this very second.

'Dear Heaven, I want you so much.' His rough voice echoed her own feelings and she shuddered against him, feeling the hard pulse of his arousal against her body. It was impossible to resist the demand of their need for one another, and Vicky moaned her assent when Jay picked her up and carried her over to the sofa. Impatiently she tugged at the buttons on his shirt, her head falling back under the scorching pressure of his mouth on her throat, roaming fiercely over her skin, finding and devouring the aching fullness of her breasts,

while her fingers struggled with his belt and zip,
her body one long silent scream of frustration until
she felt the glorious male weight of him pressing
her down into the cushions.

They made love quickly, thirstily, desperately.
hungry for one another. The moment his body
touched hers Vicky cried out as the frantic
spiralling pleasure built up inside her and
immediately he was within her, filling her, making
her writhe and twist beneath him as his mouth
burned her skin and her nails raked fiercely over
his back. It was only his mouth on hers that
silenced the wild cry of pleasure that rose to her
lips, the sledgehammer thud of his heart mirroring
the excitement of her own as his body moved
fiercely within her and the rising need for
fulfilment made her cling and incite a semi-
violence within him as she responded to his urgent
thrusts.

It was over all too quickly, her body quiescent
only briefly, his thick, muttered, 'I know . . . I
know,' soothing something of the ache that still
throbbed through her body. She shuddered as his
mouth touched her breasts and pulled away from
him, hurriedly pulling on her clothes. It seemed
unbearably cruel that tonight she could not lie
next to him, able to turn to him.

'If that's what abstaining for a couple of weeks
does to us,' he grimaced ruefully as he dressed,
'then God knows what state I'm going to be in by
the time we marry.'

'No,' Vicky agreed, suppressing a sudden stab of
pain. 'Somehow you don't strike me as a man who
would enjoy celibacy . . .'

'Then you'd be wrong.' He looked at her quite
seriously. 'There've been times when I've gone

months without a woman and scarcely even been aware of it. It's you who makes me like this . . . turns me on to such an extent that I'm in a constant state of arousal; not sex.'

It was one of the most flattering things he'd said to her, and quite unexpectedly tears stung her eyes. That he should be able to affect her emotionally so much frightened her, but then she told herself she was being foolish. They were going to be married and there was no reason for her to hide her feelings from him. Going up to him she placed her mouth against his and kissed him lingeringly, withdrawing to murmur softly in his ear. 'Jay Brentford, I think I love you . . .'

'I hope you always will,' Jay responded huskily kissing her back, and releasing her slowly. She could sense the controlled tension in his body, and rejoiced in his desire for her.

'I can see no reason why not.' And although she did not know it, they were the most foolishly trusting words she had ever uttered.


'Let me look at you.'

Suppressing a grin at the bossy tone of her daughter's voice, Vicky duly stood up for her and did a slow twirl.

Her newly washed hair hung down to her shoulders in soft curls, the make-up she had bought highlighting the unusual colour of her eyes and the delicacy of her bone structure. In the light of her bedside lamp her earrings glittered as though they were real, and the sensation of the pure silk stockings against her skin reminded her in some ways of the sensual touch of Jay's fingers.

'What do you think?'

'You look like a picture out of a magazine,' Julie breathed, plainly impressed. Vicky laughed and hugged her. 'Now promise me you'll be good for your babysitter and no staying up too late.'

Jay was waiting for her downstairs and his brief silence when she walked into the room, coupled with the glinting appreciation that darkened his eyes, made her extravagance well worth while.

'You were undeniably attractive before,' he told her, while he helped her on with her jacket. 'But like this ... Are you sure you want to go to this dinner party?'

'And waste all my finery if we don't?' she mocked. The blaze of desire in his eyes had already excited her and she knew that he was aware of it. Under cover of helping her with her jacket, his hands found and cupped her breasts, and she could feel her nipples grow tight and hard.

When he stepped away from her his was the smile that was mocking. 'We won't be too late,' he assured their babysitter.

Vicky was well aware of Mrs Mayh's speculative curiosity about them, and was amused by it. Tonight they were going to tell Philip and his wife about their plans and no doubt by Christmas Eve it would be all over the village.

Philip himself opened the door to them, and Vicky could see that he was surprised to see Jay, but he covered it well.

'Go into the drawing room,' he told them. 'Mary is in there, but Christine is still upstairs. She won't be long, though.'

'Christine and I were at university at the same time,' Vicky explained to Jay, 'although we weren't in the same year. She's been living in the States for some time now.'

'Vicky, my dear, how lovely you look,' Mary greeted her, 'and . . .'

'Jay Brentford, Mrs Sterne,' Jay introduced himself smoothly, 'Vicky's fiancé.'

'Fiancé!' Philip came in just in time to catch Jay's announcement and was plainly stunned.

'Vicky, you never said . . .'

'It's all happened so quickly that neither of us has taken it in properly ourselves yet,' Jay interrupted, smiling at him.

And it was Jay who answered Mary's excited questions about their marriage and when it was to take place. 'So soon,' Vicky heard her breathe. 'My . . . that certainly is quick work.'

'Well there's no reason for either of us to wait, I . . .' He broke off as the door opened. Vicky recognised Christine at once, although she was wearing her hair in a different style and her clothes were far more sophisticated than the jeans and sweater she had worn during her university days. Her companion was unfamiliar to Vicky; a tall, dark-haired man in his late thirties, who was introduced as Christine's husband.

'We thought we'd better come over now, because Ian plans that by this time next year, there'll be three of us and not just two,' Christine grinned.

'Christine you haven't met Vicky's fiancé, Jay, yet,' her mother interrupted, plainly a little flustered by her daughter's open reference to the prospect of a grandchild, as yet not conceived.

'Yes,' Christine smiled extending her hand to Jay. 'I recognised you, of course. How wildly romantic. How on earth did the two of you get together again, or have you always kept in touch? I'll never forget the expression on your face,

Vicky,' she added, turning to Vicky and smiling reminiscently, 'the first time you set eyes on Jay. It was at one of Roger Howell's parties,' she explained to her parents. 'You know how shy poor Vicky was, well we managed to persuade her to come with us ... and when Jay walked in she just stood there staring at him like someone poleaxed. And I might say the attraction wasn't all one sided,' she added with a laugh. 'Jay walked straight over to her and before any of us knew what was happening, there they were dancing together. Where on earth did the two of you get to? I didn't see you for days after that ... whoops, tactless of me!'

Vicky wasn't listening. She felt as though she had just been plunged into fathoms of icy water. The shock to her system was so great that she was not aware of anything but the appalling, unbelievable, horror of what Christine had just revealed. Numbly she looked across at Jay and read in his eyes the truth of Christine's revelation. Nausea clawed sickly and violently at her stomach; and she suffered the most acute sensation of degradation and self-loathing. She wanted to tear off the restraining hand Jay had placed on her shoulder as though he knew of her intense desire to get away from him ... from everyone in this room.

Around her she could hear the others talking, laughing ... and like an automaton she was distantly aware of them, but the only reality for her was the immense horror of what Christine had so unwittingly revealed. Jay ... was the twins' father ... Jay was the man who had ... Jay the one she had drunkenly given her body to. Of all the appalling, bitter coincidences. It seemed impossible that the whole thing was not some cruel jest. Perhaps it was, Vicky acknowledged sickly, but the jester in that case must surely be fate. Now, suddenly she remembered Jay talking about friends of his in Bristol, but how on earth could she have known those friends had such a relevance in her own past . . .? And she had wanted him. The sick desolation of it crucified her. How could she have wanted this man? She started to shiver, and opened her mouth to say that she had to leave, but Jay's fingers tightened warningly round her arm.

'Let go of me.' She whispered it frantically, shrinking back when he turned her into his body and said quietly, shielding her from the others. 'For God's sake try and pull yourself together. There's nothing we can do now. We'll talk about it later. I know you've had a shock . . .'

A shock. A hysterical laugh bubbled up inside her, shut off as she felt the warmth of his breath searing her skin. It burned like a brand, increasing her feeling of sick loathing. And yet he was right; much as she wanted to she could hardly just walk out.

The meal was a nightmare, but she left it to Jay to play her part in the dinner table conversation.

The meal came to an end with her having no notion of what she had had to eat or drink, with no notion of anything apart from the truth beating through her brain. Jay. Jay was the one . . . How on earth hadn't she recognised him? Why hadn't she known? With shaming agony she knew why; because she had been too drunk to remember what her ravisher looked like. Too drunk and too desperate for him to make love to her . . . Unwanted the memory of the fierce excitement pulsing through her when they danced, surged through her; the same excitement he engendered in her now. She couldn't bear it. She closed her eyes, suddenly conscious of Jay's voice in her ear.

'For God's sake pull yourself together,' he muttered. 'Do you want them to guess that . . .?'

'That what?' she asked bitterly, cutting across him, 'That you raped me?'

She felt as though the evening would never be over. Dear Christ the irony of it . . . the care and pleasure with which she had selected this outfit, wanting Jay to look at her and find her desirable. Now she shrank from so much as the lightest touch of his hand against her arm.

'Vicky, my dear, you've been so quiet,' Mary commented, frowning slightly when they were at last able to leave. 'Are you all right?'

'A headache,' she lied briefly, 'nothing to worry about. I hope I haven't spoiled your party.'

Jay's fingers round her arm once they were outside warned her of the futility of trying to escape. The thick silence of the car pressed heavily down on her, threatening to suffocate her. She didn't want to go back to the house with him. She started to shake, and heard him swear savagely. 'Stop it,' he ordered thickly, turning towards her and watching her flinch. The colour left his face and then surged back, dark and angrily. 'For God's sake, don't look at me like that, I'm not going to hurt you, damn you. I can't believe it . . .' He seemed dazed, almost as shaken as she was herself, and she had to lash out at him to protect herself from him.

'No, I suppose you thought you'd left it all safely behind you, didn't you?' She laughed savagely, hating herself, her skin crawling with self-revulsion. How could she have wanted him? What was wrong with her? Was she mentally sick?

'If you knew how much time I spent trying to find you, you'd never say that,' Jay told her violently.

'Why, so that you could repeat the exercise? Gave you a taste for rape did it?'

'For God's sake listen to me ...'

'No ... whatever it is I don't want to hear it.' By what malevolent trick of fate had they not recognised one another? She wasn't aware of actually voicing the words, until Jay said tiredly, 'It was ten years ago, you had longer hair then, your face was still chubby with adolescence and I admit I didn't make much of a study of you. You were a willing body when I needed something to assuage my own pain.'

'*Your* pain ...' Her voice rose. 'You took me and you used me. I could have been anyone ...' All the bitterness of the past rose up and swamped her.

'Do you think I haven't paid for what I did?' He stopped the car abruptly and turned to face her, 'And will you stop trying to turn me into the villain of the piece? Both of us, for whatever reason, on that particular night did not behave in character, I because I had just learned that the girl I believed I loved and who I thought loved me had married someone else, and you ... because your inhibitions had been unlocked by too much drink, and whilst I admit that the greater blame is undoubtedly mine, not all of it is. It would have taken a man of stone to resist the lure you were handing out that night,' he told her brutally. 'Dear God, the way you were dancing with me was the nearest thing to making love without actually doing so that I've ever experienced.'

'Making love?' Vicky's voice was bitter. 'What

you did to me wasn't making love. It was brutal
... hateful.' A sour taste filled her mouth as she
was back in the past, remembering her own
terrified cries of denial when she finally realised
what was happening.

'You were in the wrong place at the wrong
time.' Jay's voice was tired and bleak. 'And I
admit that I was punishing you for another
woman's betrayal. I've no defence against that. I
mistook you for an eager little wanton, and I used
you accordingly. By the time I found out the truth
it was too late to do anything about it. The next
day I made enquiries about you, but Roger knew
nothing about you. He thought you must have
come with friends of his brother's.'

When she remained silent he re-started the car,
not speaking until they were back at the vicarage
once again. He had to take the babysitter home
and while he did so Vicky went upstairs and
prepared for bed, locking her door against him.

Tomorrow was Christmas Eve and he was going
to London. She never wanted him to come back.
Unable to sleep, she got up and pulled on her old
thick dressing gown, padding down the corridor to
his suite. He opened the door the moment she
knocked. He was still dressed, his face compressed
into hard lines of weariness.

'I just came to tell you that after this I never
want to set eyes on you again,' Vicky told him
emotionlessly. She saw his mouth thin and
stepped away from him. 'Don't touch me, Jay, if
you do I think I'll be sick.' Her composure
broke as she threw at him bitterly. 'Have you
any idea what it did to me to know what I'd
done ... given myself to a man who used me
like a whore, and all because I was too naïve to

realise exactly what the innocuous punch I was drinking really was?'

His face was shuttered as he looked at her. 'You're too overwrought for us to discuss this now, Vicky, we'll talk about it when I get back from London.'

'No!' The word burst from her. 'You're not going to come back. I won't let you. I never want to set eyes on you again, Jay, do you hear me!'

Somehow she managed to stumble back to her own room, where she lay crouched under the bedclothes shivering like a trapped animal, her thoughts circling one another until she was dizzy with the effort of following them. At last sleep dropped on her like a thick mantle, mercifully obliterating everything.

# CHAPTER NINE

SOMEHOW when she woke in the morning she knew that Jay had gone. She sensed it even without actually having heard him leave. The enormity of the hold he had on her emotions twisted sickeningly through her and she moaned out loud, burying her face in her pillow. How could she have wanted him? How could he have aroused her to such a frenzy of physical desire? How could her body have betrayed her so—and with him of all men? If there was any real justice in the world he ought to have been the one man who could not arouse her, not the only one who could. The sickening reality of what she was admitting engulfed her. She should loathe him, not herself ... and yet as he had reminded her last night the fact that they had been lovers was not his fault alone; she had encouraged him, wanted him, her cruelly sharp mind reminded her now, taking her back again to that ill-fated party.

Christine's words echoed painfully through her memory ... You looked poleaxed when you saw him ... and it was all too humiliatingly true. She had been drunk when Jay arrived, but not too drunk to be unaware of his male appeal, and she had acted in a way so totally out of character that even now she could hardly believe it. She had been the one to invite him to dance, moving suggestively against his body when they did that it was no wonder he had thought her wanton. She had wanted him to notice her and he had. She had wanted him to take her away and make love to her. She had wanted the fierce, primitive thrust of his body within her own. He had aroused feeling in her she had never known before—or since. Not until . . . But then the drunken mists had cleared and she had realised he was not some dashing prince joining her in her own private realisation of some adolescent daydream, but a flesh and blood man, using her body ruthlessly and uncaringly, not sharing the overwhelming attention she had felt for him at first sight but taking her because she was willing and he was in need. She had fought him then, but he had overwhelmed her, leaving her so abruptly after he had possessed her that her humiliation had increased tenfold.

In all the time since the twins' birth their father had remained a misty character in her mind, his features hidden from her so that all she could conjure up from her memory of him was the feel of his body against her own, and the sickening knowledge of what she had invited by dancing with him. Not that he had had to force her to go to that bedroom with hm. Her mouth twisted, her body tensing in rejection of what she was forcing herself to remember. When he suggested they slip away somewhere quieter together she had been all too eager to agree. The alcohol had completely stripped away her inhibitions; she had been dizzy with her sudden and powerful feelings for him; with the effect of his body moving against her own. Shudders broke out, racking her body, sweat dampening her skin, as the memories tormented her. Weakly she struggled to sit up and throw off the bedclothes. She wanted to cower underneath them and stay there—for the rest of her life. She remembered now she had felt much the same when she realised she was pregnant. Unwillingly, she remembered Jay saying he had tried to find her. Her mouth compressed. Thank God he had not. But he had found her now . . .

'Are you okay, Ma?'

The concern in Charles' voice as he called to her from outside her bedroom door reminded her that she was not eighteen any more, and now had responsibilities that could not be ignored.

'Just a bit tired,' she told him. 'I'll be down soon.'

A brisk shower helped to revive her a little, but there was nothing she could do to stop her stomach churning and her muscles locking she admitted, watching the childen eat their breakfast, while she tried to force down a slice of toast. She felt cold . . . inside and out . . .

'When will Jay be back?' Julie asked her, pausing in between spoonfuls of porridge.

Never! The word screamed through her brain, but she could not utter it. Her body seemed to be completely paralysed. What on earth was she going to tell the children? She still needed time to come to terms with what had happened herself before she could tell them anything she decided, answering Julie's question with a brief, 'I don't know.'

Was it really only yesterday that she had been so happy, so content and excited about the future? What a fool she had been. It seemed impossible now that she hadn't recognised Jay on sight or he her, but then why should they have done? She had changed from the gauche adolescent she had been at eighteen, and she doubted if he had paid much, if any, attention then to her appearance. She, too, after what had happened had blotted the features of her betrayer out of her mind not wanting to remember ... least of all how much she had physically wanted him in those first moments of seeing and watching him. Nor had she wanted to remember the thrill of excitement she had felt when her wide-eyed scrutiny of him had suddenly registered and he had come towards her, each step nearer to her, making her heart thud with erratic, crazy excitement.

'Ma ... are you okay?'

With an effort she forced a smile. 'I'm fine thanks, Charles, just a bit tired.'

God, it was so true. She wanted to go to sleep and never, ever wake up again. How could she have done that to herself? How could she have fallen for Jay? Why was the only man she could respond to be the one who ...

She became aware of the silence around the breakfast table and pulled herself out of the dark abyss of her tormented thoughts with an effort. It was Christmas Eve and if she didn't start behaving normally the children were bound to suspect something was wrong. Time enough for them to learn the truth tomorrow when Jay did not appear.

'Are we going to Midnight Mass tonight?' Charles asked her excitedly as he helped her clear away the breakfast things.

She had taken the children with her the previous year for the first time, and numbly she nodded. Perhaps in the peace and quiet of the small country church she would find some measure of salvation. She certainly needed it.

Mary rang her during the morning, enquiring about her headache, adding to her burden of guilt.

'And Jay is so charming, Vicky ... I can't tell you how delighted we are for you, my dear.'

By the time she had hung up she was shaking, tears pouring down her face. There was a weakness in her body similar to the aftermath of 'flu. Her own self-hatred would destroy her if she wasn't careful, Vicky thought. Her hatred of Jay was not and never could be as great as her loathing of herself—not because of the past so much but because of the present; because now, today, she reacted to him in a way that made her ache with self-disgust. Even last night when he touched her . . . Perspiration broke out on her skin and she was shivering at the same time. It was as though her mind and body were two separate things, her mind rejecting him, her body wantonly welcoming him, wanting him.

Despite all that she had to do the day dragged by on leaden feet. John Stafford from Lees Farm called, delivering the turkey he had promised her in return for her help with his books. It looked large enough to feed an army and she eyed it without enthusiasm. Charles' dog, who he had called Hero, barked sharply when John arrived, yapping at his heels, until she managed to quiet him down. Jay had taken the puppy for a check-up and his injections a week or so ago. When John had gone she stared blindly at the turkey and then to her own consternation suddenly burst into tears and cried until her body actually physically ached.

P.M.T. blues she told herself angrily, drying her eyes. Jay was not worth crying over; she ought to be thanking her lucky stars that she had found out in time. What manner of man was he to have done what he had to her? And then unwillingly she found herself remembering him telling her about his fiancée breaking their engagement to marry someone else. At twenty-seven she knew enough about human nature to see quite well how a man burdened with that sort of rejection could turn to someone else and take them in a mingling of fury and physical need. He had not been making love to her, he had been punishing her—or rather her whole sex—for the betrayal of one woman. Deliberately she closed her mind to her thoughts; she did not want to find excuses or explanations for him. He was gone from her life and she never wanted him back in it.

She got up and went upstairs to bathe her eyes. On her way back down again she stopped outside the door to Jay's suite. Without conscious volition her fingers were on the door handle, turning it, pushing the door open. The small sitting room was bare of any of his possessions as was the bedroom beyond. He had gone, just as she had told him to do. So why did she have this tight knot of pain inside? She knew quite well why . . . because she loved him. Wildly, improbable though it was, the fact was there. But how could she love a man who had done what he had and still retain her self-respect?

Once again she reminded herself that the judgment she had made of him at eighteen was not the same one she would have made now, but her aching heart refused to be appeased. She had thought him a white knight out of a childhood dream and he had smashed that dream beyond repair, leaving her alone to face the appalling consequences of their union. Except—he had tried to find her . . .

She spent the afternoon wrapping the children's presents. When they came in for tea they were under the tree. She could feel their excitement, but for once it eluded her. Pain surrounded her like an unburstable bubble.

As she got ready for Midnight Mass, every movement seemed a terrible effort. She didn't want to go, but she must. If she stayed here alone with her thoughts ... She shivered, shaking violently, the full nature of her loss suddenly crashing down on her. She loved Jay and she had sent him away, but what other alternative had she had? To live with him would mean spending her life hating herself for caring so deeply for him.

The sound of carols floated all around her as she stood in church with Charles, Julie and Jamie, but she was not part of the service. She was not part of anything any more. She felt light-headed—unreal—as though the world had slipped out of focus and she was no longer quite part of it.

'Ma, are you all right?' Charles asked anxiously as they were driven home by Philip Sterne. 'In church I thought you were going to faint.'

She gave him a reassuring smile, and then reminded herself that she hadn't eaten all day, and that that was probably the reason she felt so strange.

The house was ominously dark when they got back. Philip dropped them at the end of the drive and she saw Charles and the twins searching the drive as they walked up it and knew they were looking for Jay's car.

'Jay isn't back,' Charles said, his obvious disappointment confirming her thoughts. 'Never mind. He'll be here for tomorrow.'

His blind faith hurt her. She had seen the burdens of worry slip off his shoulders since they had told him they were going to get married. He was becoming a teenage boy instead of a miniature adult. Now ...

Surprisingly she actually slept and was woken

by Jamie jumping on her bed, with the stocking she had placed at the end of his.

'Happy Christmas, Ma . . .'

Julie joined him and their combined weight warmed her. Her children . . . Jay's children she thought, her heart almost stopping beating. She looked at them with new eyes, seeing him clearly in them now. They had his strong dark hair and his grey eyes.

'Aren't you going to get up?' Julie demanded plaintively. 'I'm hungry.'

What point was there in staying in bed?

The twins were noisily exuberant over breakfast, playing with the puzzles she had put in their stockings, while Charles read the computer book she had bought him on the performance of the BBC Micro.

After they had cleared everything away and washed up, Vicky walked towards the sitting room, checked by Julie who said suddenly. 'Ma, we can't open our other presents now, Jay isn't here yet.'

The hall swayed blackly around her, and she took a deep breath.

Now . . . she would have to tell them now. She opened her mouth and then the words were suspended in frozen disbelief in her brain as Julie shrieked out. 'Here he is now . . . I can hear the car!'

She couldn't believe it. All three children charged to the front door while she hung back. It couldn't be Jay . . . he wouldn't . . . not after what had happened.

But it was. In a dream she watched him emerge from the car, brushing snowflakes from his face as the promise of snow forecast that morning became reality. The children beseiged him, the twins dancing round him like exuberant puppies. He picked Julie up swinging her into his arms until her face was level with his and then kissed her. Across the few yards that separated them his eyes met hers and Vicky saw quite clearly in them the message. Mine ... he was telling her ... they're mine. Unwittingly she shrank back, aware as she had been last night in church of a sense of being cut off ... apart from the rest of mankind.

Jay was opening the boot of his car, pulling out a suitcase.

'Hurry, hurry,' Julie exhorted excitedly. 'We haven't opened our presents yet, we've been waiting for you.'

And as he came into the hall suddenly the house seemed alive, as though it, too, had been waiting ...

'I'll go and make some coffee, the rest of you go into the sitting room.'

She turned quickly, shivering with nerves and shock. She knew without turning round that he was behind her. As he closed the kitchen door she heard him say to the children, 'If you look in the boot you'll find a parcel for each of you. Your mother and I will be with you in a moment.'

'I told you not to come back.'

She said it without emotion, busying herself with the task of making coffee. It gave her something to do with her hands and an excuse not to look at him.

'But surely you didn't think I wouldn't?'

'I suppose I ought to have known.' Her voice was thick with anger. 'You never were a man who paid any attention to someone else's wishes when they differed from your own.'

She had to turn round to reach the coffee beans, and the stark pallor of his face shocked her, breaking through her own aching pain briefly.

'I know what you're getting at,' he told her flatly. 'Look, Vicky, I was as shocked as you were the other night, but I tried to tell you then. What happened between us, what I did, was completely out of character for me. I had only just that afternoon heard from Jenny that she was marrying someone else. I'd been invited to the party that morning by John. He worked for the firm of solicitors I'd been dealing with. I was still in shock ... half out of my mind with it ... I used you because of Jenny, I can't deny that but neither can I wrap it in pretty ribbon and make it acceptable and I'm not going to try. But what you can believe is that when sanity reasserted itself, I looked high and low for you ... I asked John if he knew who you were, but he didn't; the university crowd you'd been with had all dispersed and gone their various ways.'

That much had been true. The party had been by way of an-end-of-term celebration, combined with a birthday party for their host's elder brother—Jay's acquaintance no doubt.

'John was curious enough as it was when I asked about you, I could hardly tell him why I wanted to find you. Not because of myself,' he added harshly when he saw her face, 'I was thinking of you. I didn't think you would want it bandied around that you'd been to bed with a complete stranger. You see by then it had occurred to me that since you had been a virgin ... Oh hell,' he exploded, 'don't look at me like that ... you came on pretty strong to me, you can't deny that ...'

'And so it was all my fault,' Vicky countered evenly. Against her will she was forced to accept the logic of what he was saying. To see herself and what had happened through his eyes instead of her own, but she didn't want to let herself.

'Can't you understand that even now I'm finding it hard to take it all in? The twins are mine, of course?'

'Don't worry, I'm not about to ask you for maintenance for them.'

His mouth went grim. 'You won't have to,' he told her silkily. 'When you're my wife I shall support them as a matter of course.'

His *wife*. Did he think she was mad? She was just about to demand an explanation when the door burst open and Jamie rushed in, his hair ruffled into spikes, his eyes sparkling with excited disbelief.

'Jay's bought me a BMX,' he told Vicky, half stammering in his pleasure. 'Come and look at it.'

She had little alternative but to follow him into the sitting room, the floor already strewn with torn paper. The BMX, shining new, was propped up against the sofa.

Furiously Vicky stared from the bike to Jay.

'I bought it before any of this happened,' he told her quietly.

'Ma . . . look at this.' Charles had removed the paper from his present and was staring bemused at the computer he had wanted. A rage of sickness filled her throat as Vicky watched Jay crouch down on the floor to talk to Charles about it. He was buying them, she told herself bitterly, buying her children's affection, but common sense told her that was not true. Even so it hurt desperately to see the pleasure in the boys' eyes as they admired the gifts she had known they wanted, but also had known she could never, ever have afforded. She would have liked to have been the one to put that pleasure into their eyes.

'You're very generous,' she said tonelessly to Jay when he came back to join her by the door. 'My presents will seem very tame after these.'

She saw the flush of colour stain his cheek-bones and felt his leashed anger, but all he said was, 'That wasn't my intention.'

Almost instantly she felt ashamed of herself. She turned her face away.

What had he bought Julie? She soon knew, watching the flush of pleasure colour her daughter's face as she brought over to show her a complete set of matching co-ordinated pre-teenage wear. Julie was only just beginning to take an interest in fashion, and the bright coloured cotton and wool separates Jay had chosen for her would tempt the soul of any young girl.

'I just hope they're the right size,' Jay commented when Julie was back on the floor admiring Charles' computer. 'The saleswoman seemed to think they would be.'

With the children opening the rest of their presents there was no opportunity for them to talk. Vicky sat at the dinner table, almost in a trance, letting the excited hub of conversation flow over her, her skin chilling every time she remembered what Jay had said to her. There was no way she was going to marry him now. He must know that . . .

It was evening before they were alone. The children had gone to bed quite early, without the usual protests, and Vicky came downstairs from saying her good nights, to find Jay waiting on the bottom stair for her.

'I'm tired, Jay,' she told him, avoiding his eyes. 'I want to go to bed myself.'

'Not before we've talked.'

'There's nothing to talk about. I asked you not to come back here . . . and I wish you hadn't.'

'The twins are my children, Vicky.'

How could she deny it?

'Children you didn't know existed until a couple of days ago,' she managed to retort, tensing as he took her arm and led her into the sitting room. She was too tired to resist or move away, and it shocked her that her body should react so vibrantly to his proximity. She should be shrinking from him in loathing not . . . not what? Not anything, she told herself firmly, closing her mind against the truth. Not anything at all.

'But now that I do, I want some say in their upbringing. You're cutting your nose off to spite them, Vicky,' he warned her. 'There are many financial advantages that I could give them.'

'I won't marry you.'

'Oh, yes, you will,' he told her evenly, 'because if you don't, I intend to do everything I can to assert my legal rights to my children.'

Shock engulfed her and she stared disbelievingly up at him. 'That . . . that's blackmail! You . . . you wouldn't . . .'

'Wouldn't I? I assure you that I would.'

'But why?'

'You made a commitment to marry me, Vicky, and I'm not going to let you welch on that. The discovery that I'm the children's natural father might have changed your desire to marry me, but it hasn't altered mine to marry you. I still want you as my wife, and I think that once you're over

the shock of discovering the truth, you'll be glad
that I forced the issue.'

His self-confidence astounded and infuriated
her. 'Never,' she told him vehemently, 'Never!'

His mouth thinned warningly, 'But you will
marry me, my dear, be very sure of that.'

He would carry his threat of trying to take the
children away from her through, Vicky knew that.
Perhaps after all the loss of his first fiancée to
someone else had left a residue of bitterness.

'Give in, Vicky, you've no other alternative.'

It was true, she hadn't. How could she tell the
children now that she wasn't going to marry him?
Today had proved how much they loved him.

'Why are you doing this?' she demanded
fiercely, hating herself for knowing she must give
way.

'Many reasons, including the fact that I still want
you—very much.'

Her shock showed in her eyes, and he laughed,
and said softly. 'Oh yes . . . very, very much . . .'

He actually expected her to live with him as his
wife after what had happened? She could scarcely
take it in.

And then suddenly on a stomach churning wave
of feeling she knew what she must do.

'Very well then, Jay,' she told him quietly,
avoiding his eyes, 'I will marry you.'

Watching the triumph glitter in his eyes when
she eventually forced herself to meet them, she
added mentally, 'but I will never, ever physically
be your wife.' She wasn't going to tell him that
now. She'd save it . . . for a wedding present.

# CHAPTER TEN

THEY were married very quietly three days after Christmas by special licence. The children were overjoyed and looking round the few guests attending their small wedding breakfast, Vicky suspected that she was the only person there, for whatever reason, to take absolutely no pleasure in their marriage.

She had kept Jay at a distance ever since she had agreed to it, shutting him out of her heart and her mind with an ice-cold determination that she would allow nothing to pierce.

'My dear, you look pale, are you all right?'

She smiled briefly at Mary's concern, wondering what the older woman would say if she told her the truth. The wedding breakfast had been Mary's idea, and Jay had backed her up in it, as much because he knew how much she would hate it as for any other reason, Vicky suspected.

'I'm fine. It's all just been such a rush.'

'Yes, but now you can relax,' Mary's smile was sympathetic, 'and don't worry about the children, we'll take good care of them.'

'Yes ... I know you will.' Her response was automatic. This honeymoon respite from the children's presence that Jay had organised for them was the last thing she wanted, but she had been unable to dissuade him. They both needed a chance to relax, he had told her. In the New Year they would start looking for another house; there was a great deal for both of them to do. Having got his own way in forcing her to marry him, he seemed to have put the reason for her reluctance right out of his mind, and behaved towards her just as he had done before they had learned the truth about the past. His lover-like attitude grated on her too-finely tuned nerves, edged as she suspected it to be with a fine mockery.

'Ready to go?'

Although she had not acknowledged him she had been well aware that Jay had come to stand behind her. It gave her a perverse kind of pleasure to pretend that she was unaware of him—a way of punishing herself as well as him for the fact that she was. And it was that very awareness that kept the shadows in her eyes and her appetite non-existent, her nerves strung so tight she was sometimes afraid they might actually snap. No matter how much she tried to evade or escape the truth, it kept on returning to torment her. And it was that weakness that she hated so much in herself that she needed to punish Jay for, for being the one to reveal it. It lacerated her self-respect to ribbons to know the truth and she hated herself for it.

She smiled thinly at him now, knowing he would see the hatred burning in her eyes, even if no one else did.

'Why not?'

She said goodbye to the twins and Charles, warning them to behave themselves while they were in Mary's care. They were only going away for a few days. Jay had booked them a suite at the Dorchester, and Mary had sighed enviously when he explained that he wanted Vicky to enjoy a few days' spoiling before they set about house-hunting.

They left in a shower of goodbye cries, the

twins' beaming faces the last ones to disappear as Jay's car turned the corner of the drive.

This was the moment she had been dreading since he had forced her into agreeing to marry him. Up until now, she had managed to work things so that they were rarely completely alone—and certainly never for more than the odd ten minutes or so. Now the long drive to London stretched intimidatingly ahead of her. She leaned back in her seat, closing her eyes. The hat Mary had insisted she purchase for the wedding was lying on the back seat, a small cap of winter white wool with a fetching stiffened black net brim. Her winter white wool dress with its matching jacket set off the brilliance of her hair, but as she closed her eyes Vicky was completely uninterested in her appearance. She had dressed for the wedding like a mechanical doll. It had even been too much of an effort to pack a going away case—Mary had done that for her, although God alone knew what on earth she could have found in her wardrobe that was suitable for a sophisticated London hotel, Vicky reflected grimly.

A little to her surprise Jay made no attempt to talk to her. On Boxing Day he had made an attempt, but she had rebuffed him by the simple expedient of getting up and walking out of the room. Since then they had behaved towards one another as polite strangers, but she suspected that Jay was merely biding his time and that it wasn't a state of affairs he was prepared to allow to go on indefinitely.

Well, the confrontation could not come soon enough for her. Tonight she would tell him that she was not prepared to sleep with him, to share his bed and allow him access to her body. He had overruled her decision not to marry him, and if he didn't like the price he was going to have to pay for getting his own way, well he was just going to have to, because there was no way she was going to change her mind.

Deep down inside her Vicky knew that she was not only punishing Jay but also punishing herself for ever having wanted him. In her anguish she wanted to crush and destroy every sensation he had ever aroused in her, to obliterate them as though they had never been.

His lack of desire to communicate with her, at first surprising became slightly nerve-racking by the time they reached the motorway. It wasn't a happy silence; it was a startling, electric, tense one. She could feel the tension gripping her muscles and as the miles sped by, she became aware of the fact that she was clenching her jaw, tensing her stomach. She wouldn't look at Jay ... to do so would in some subtle way be to give in to him. She tried to relax by breathing slowly, closing her eyes and willing her mind to empty. She had hardly slept since Christmas Eve but she didn't want to now. She had gone beyond mere tiredness to a point where her nervous tension was keeping her keyed up and alert.

They reached the city centre, Jay's easy familiarity with their route reminding her of the life he had here. Did he still intend to delegate his work? She frowned, checking the thought ... checking any thought that led towards him in any sort of way.

On the gloomy winter afternoon, the reception area of the Dorchester was warmly welcoming. Jay was given the key to their suit by a smiling receptionist and Vicky trailed slowly behind him in

the direction of one of the lifts. He had obviously
made previous arrangements about the garaging of
his car, because a member of the hotel staff had
driven it away after the uniformed commissionaire
had escorted them from it.

They weren't the only ones to step into the lift.
It purred swiftly upward, stopping abruptly. Vicky
rocked slightly on her heels, tensing in rejection as
Jay's hand came out to steady her, her eyes
flashing bitter sparks of dislike.

'This is our floor.'

Mutely she followed him out of the lift and down
what seemed like miles of thickly carpeted corridor.

Outside one of the doors Jay stopped and
inserted the key, holding back to allow her to
precede him. As she did so her jacket brushed
against his and she grimaced in distaste. Fleetingly
she was aware of a dark burning anger in his eyes
as they meshed with hers. It gave her a heady
feeling of pleasure. So she had pierced his arrogant
armour. Good! *Good*, she thought savagely, let
him suffer a little.

The sitting room of their suite overlooked the
park. It was elegantly furnished with classic taste.
The walls were painted a soft blue, the panel
mouldings picked out in white. A softly hued
Chinese rug covered the polished floor, with two
settees and a chair, upholstered in toning polished
cotton, to relax in. In front of one of the windows
was a writing desk, and opposite a television. A
fireplace decorated one wall, flanked by shelves. In
spite of herself Vicky was impressed by the room's
elegance, but she wasn't going to say so.

On the furthest wall was a door and Jay strode
over to it, opening it; Vicky could see into a small
corridor with another door off it.

A brief tap on the door signalled the arrival of their luggage. While Jay went to tip the porter, Vicky examined the bedroom.

The bed was huge, the headboard and other furniture gilded in a French Empire style. From a coronet fixed in the ceiling, heavy satin drapes fell round the top of the bed. The room was decorated in soft peach and coffee tones, the thick peach carpet inches deep. Jay was still in the sitting room, and Vicky wandered through into their private bathroom. It was huge and old-fashioned, but very elegant. The bath was large enough for a family, she reflected, staring at it, admiring the timeless Edwardian lavishness of the fittings. Small bottles of Molton Brown products were provided on a glass shelf, everything from body shampoo to moisturiser. There was more storage space in their bedroom than she had at home. Her few clothes would be lost in it.

'Would you like something to drink?'

Jay moved so quietly for such a tall man that if she hadn't known of his presence from the atavistic prickle at the back of her neck she would never have known he was there.

'We've got our own bar, or I can get room service if you prefer tea or coffee. Failing that we could always go downstairs and have afternoon tea. They make quite a thing of it here.'

For a moment she compared the solitude and privacy of their suite to the bustle of one of the public rooms and then made her choice. 'Afternoon tea, I think,' she said coolly, and she knew from the grim expression in Jay's eyes that he knew exactly why she had made that choice.

'As you wish, but all you're doing is putting off what we both know must happen, eventually,' he told her suavely. Vicky took a deep breath. Now was the time ... but not here in the bedroom. She moved ahead of him into the sitting room and stood in front of the window, hands clasped in front of her as she stared out of the window before turning to face him.

For a moment her heart almost stopped beating. He was standing in the doorway, watching her lazily, the angle of his body stretching the fine silk of his shirt over his chest, revealing the pattern of body hair beneath it.

Against her will she was reminded of how his skin had felt beneath her hands, hot and faintly moist, his body strong and yet at the same time vulnerable, his breathing harsh as he made love to her.

Forcing down the too intrusive memory she said coolly, 'Jay, I married you because I had no alternative, but I want you to know that although I may be your wife in name, I will never be so in body.'

For a moment there was silence, and then he said pleasantly. 'How very predictable you are, Vicky. Somehow I thought you might come up with something like this.' He looked at her and laughed cynically. 'My dear, how can you stand there and tell me that when we both know how you respond to me?'

It brought colour to her too pale skin, but she had been prepared for this sort of ploy and had armoured herself against it.

'Once,' she agreed with a calmness she was having to force. 'But not now.'

She held her breath not sure what to expect, but willing him to understand that she meant every word she was saying.

'I see.' His mouth was grim, almost frighteningly so and for a moment she was terrified that he would ignore what she had said ... that he would come to her and take her regardless of her wishes. The twist of sensation deep inside her widened her eyes in shock and left her shaking inwardly with physical sickness as she fought against the knowledge that some part of her actually wanted ... what? To be forced? No, not that, but perhaps to be overruled ... that same wanton sick part of her that had led her into this mess in the first place.

'Well, I suppose we might as well go down and have that afternoon tea.'

His easy acceptance of her ultimatum staggered her. She had expected at least some token argument. As they descended to the public area of the hotel in the lift she was stricken with a sudden suspicion. Perhaps he had not married her because he wanted her after all. Perhaps it had only been the twins he had wanted ... he had threatened her with legal action to get them, but as they were illegitimate it would have been a hard struggle for him to succeed and she had given way to protect the twins themselves more than anything else. But wasn't he in a much stronger position to take them from her, now, if he so wished?

She was so consumed with fear that she barely touched the tempting delicacies provided for their afternoon tea. Jay on the other hand seemed to have a good appetite, at one point leaning across to her and murmuring dulcetly, 'What's the matter? Is it something of a pyrrhic victory, my love?'

It brought her back to reality. She was letting her fears get too strong a hold on her. Coolly ignoring him she turned instead to study the people around them, family groups in the main, the mothers elegantly clothed and be-furred, diamonds twinkling discreetly in ear lobes and at throats and wrists.

'Since our honeymoon is not likely to include any of the more usual pleasures, may I suggest that you spend some time re-equipping your wardrobe,' Jay suggested, derisively following her gaze. 'As my wife you will be expected to dress accordingly.'

Her eyes flashed, but she could not argue, not in the face of the implacable determination she could read in his eyes. He wanted to humiliate her, she thought sickly . . . and if he couldn't do it sexually then he would find another way.

'How will you occupy your time?' That should make it clear to him that she neither wanted nor intended to have his company.

'There's a well-equipped gym in the basement here, plus a swimming pool, and I've brought some work with me,' he told her blandly. 'I shan't lack occupations to pass my time.' As he spoke he was looking across at a table where two women sat on their own. The younger of them was superbly dressed; model thin with high cheek-bones and blonde hair. As though aware of Jay's scrutiny she looked across at him and smiled.

A bitter fury rose in Vicky's throat like gall. Underneath their table her fingers clenched into her palms, but she refused to let Jay see what she was feeling.

That evening they dined, at Jay's insistence, in their suite. They were both tired, he told her curtly, and he for one wanted an early night.

Vicky wanted to refuse to share the bed with

him, but a little to her confusion he went to bed first, and when eventually she plucked up the courage to go through into the bedroom, he was fast asleep.

The bed was wide enough for her to maintain her distance from him. She slept with her back to him, crossly aware of the fact that she was far more aware of him than he was of her. When she woke up in the morning he had already left their suite. In the sitting room she found a note from him saying that he had gone down to the gym. There was a credit card in her name beside it, and what appeared to Vicky to be an enormous amount of cash.

It galled her to do what he said and go out shopping, but what alternative had she? If she stayed and Jay returned to the suite he might take it as an indication that she was having second thoughts and that she now wanted his company.

She stayed out all day, exhausting herself exploring Harrods and Harvey Nichols, but buying very little.

She lunched alone in Harvey Nichols, playing with her food, returning to the hotel at five o'clock.

She was both cold and tired when she reached their suite, and while she told herself that she was glad that there was no sign of Jay, nor any note to indicate where he might be, in reality she felt both miserable and alone.

She had a bath and, feeling too tired to even think about preparing for the evening, wrapped herself in the thick towelling robe provided by the hotel and went to lie down on one of the sofas to watch television.

It was the click of the lock that eventually woke

her, her mind muzzy with sleep as she stretched and lifted her head. What time was it?

She glanced at her watch, shocked to discover it was almost nine. That's what she got for not sleeping properly for so long. And Jay ... where had he been until this time? His hair was damp she realised as she looked at him, assimilating the tautness of his body in its covering tracksuit. He looked fit and healthy, his skin bronzed, in comparison she felt almost anaemic.

'I came back about four but you weren't here.' He walked over to their private bar and unlocked it, taking out a can of fruit juice. 'I went for a swim and then a run in the park.'

She could smell the clean cold evening air on him now.

'How very energetic of you.' She hadn't realised she had it in her to be so sarcastic.

'It's extremely therapeutic—perhaps you ought to try it, helps get rid of tension.'

Vicky stared at him. What was he implying?

'What do you fancy doing for dinner?'

How could he behave as though everything were normal between them?

'Nothing.' She turned her head away from him. 'I'm not hungry.'

There was a curious silence and then he said coolly, his voice soft with a dangerous menace. 'Now I, on the other hand, find that I have a considerable appetite, and you, my love, are beginning to make me very angry. You're behaving like a child, and that being the case, perhaps I ought to treat you like one and punish you accordingly.'

Before she could stop him he was picking her up off the sofa and striding through into the bedroom with her. The lamp she had switched on cast a warm glow over the room, but Vicky wasn't aware of it. Despite his outward calm, she could feel the anger beating through Jay as he dropped her on to the bed, following her there, and pinning her on to the mattress in spreadeagled imprisonment as she fought to be free of his constraining hands.

'How dare you do this to me?' she fumed bitterly, beating his chest with her fists. 'How dare you treat me like this?' And then as she looked into his eyes and saw the darkness gathering there she knew she had pushed him too far, and genuine fear quaked through her. 'You wouldn't dare,' she breathed huskily, amending her protest to, 'No! Jay . . . not again.'

They were the last words she had the energy to speak for a long time. His hands seemed to be everywhere, tugging off her protective wrap, shedding his own clothes, forstalling all her desperate writhing attempts to escape. The harsh hiss of his breath when at last he imprisoned her flaying hands and leaned over her to study the curves of her body made her shudder in violent repudiation. He wanted her. She could both see it and sense it, and she thrust violently against his constraining grasp, until she realised that her actions were further arousing him and that he was enjoying the heaving thrust of her breasts as she fought for breath.

Terror made her skin break out in a thin film of perspiration. Jay bent towards her, and she closed her eyes tensing against him, already anticipating the sensation of his mouth against her breast . . . anticipating and rejecting it while inside she shuddered on the exquisitely fine line that divides pain and pleasure. But it wasn't her breast that felt the warm moistness of his mouth, but the valley between, his tongue capturing the tiny dot of sweat that had gathered there.

Vicky shuddered in violent reaction despite her determination not to do so, her eyes wild with hatred and pain as he smiled into them.

'You want me.' He said it softly, without expression. She shook her head, vehemently denying it, hating the soft, soundless laugh that escaped him as he slid his hand along one quivering thigh and then bent his head.

She cried out in anguish and humiliation as his tongue invaded, stroked, aroused, and finally conquered the most intimate part of her, her shuttered mind springing open unleashing against her her own love for him. Before she knew it she was gasping his name between sobbing breaths, powerless to stop her body's overriding demand for satisfaction.

As unstoppable as one of Nature's most violent storms, sensation gathered and coalesced inside her, driving her, possessing her. She reached out and touched him, hungering for his maleness, feeling the fierce surge of pleasure rock him as she found him. The raw heat of his mouth against the aching peaks of her breasts at first eased and then increased their aroused ache. Beneath his supporting arm her body arched, her throat constricting on husky whimpers of pleasure as his mouth scorched her skin.

Their bodies clung damply together, the rapid thud of his heart echoing the pulsing of his body against her. Her body was slick with sweat, aching and shivering as though she were in the grip of a fever, but she couldn't move away from him. She craved his touch . . . ached for the sensation of his mouth against her body, even where it already throbbed with pain from the savagery of his passion. She was hopelessly, completely out of control, touching him, wanting him, her bottom lip almost bitten through in her effort to stop herself from crying out to him to possess her; torn apart by the sensual storm he was forcing her to share with him. It seemed no part of her body was untouched by his mouth and hands, no part of her soul inviolate from the fires he had caused to rage inside her. His breathing sounded harsh and unsteady in her ear, his tongue sending shooting flares of ecstasy along her nerve endings as it caressed the delicate convolutions of her ear. He was breathing hard, his chest crushing her breasts as it rose and fell spasmodically. Her body shuddered, mindlessly voluptuous as his mouth touched her throat; the swollen sensitivity of her aching nipples, the flat smoothness of her stomach and then beyond, making her explode with singing pleasure and reach for him to rake her nails across his flat belly and sink her teeth into his skin. The harsh sound that left his throat echoed her own feelings, her body eagerly accommodating him as he pulled her beneath him, entering her fiercely and deeply until her flesh contracted and expanded rhythmically around him, matching the increasing desperation of the breath exhaled from her tortured lungs.

Jay's mouth locked on hers, his body dominating the feverish convulsions that tormented her.

It was too much, far too much for anyone to bear. Her nails raked his skin, her body arching to the command of his, her senses absorbing the brilliant explosion of mutual pleasure; registering the harsh sob of Jay's breath as he buried his face in her shoulder.

She still ached, but now it was with the heaviness of physical satiation, too exhausted to even murmur a protest when Jay moved, pulling her body into his arms, reaching past her to switch off the lamp and pull the covers up over them.

It was still dark when she woke up, but she remembered exactly what had happened. She tried to move and found she couldn't. Jay's arm lay against her waist, his fingers tightening into her skin.

'No . . .' His voice was crisp and firm. 'No Vicky, now we're going to talk.'

'What about? Your undeniable physical powers? Your ability to reduce me to mindless begging?' Her voice rose as she spoke, her body trembling in agitation. She tensed as Jay moved and switched on the lamp. His face was pale, his mouth thinning slightly as he looked down at her, and then he said quietly, 'And don't you know yet that you have exactly the same effect on me? That your lightest touch can send me almost mindless with wanting?'

'No.' She whispered rather than spoke her denial.

'Yes,' he told her fiercely. 'Yes. Vicky listen to me. I can't wipe out the past for you . . .'

'It makes me sick to even think about it,' she told him thickly. 'I hate myself for the way I respond to you, for wanting you and loving you.'

'I know.'

'You treated me like . . .'

His fingers closed her lips. 'Don't say it, please . . . I've tried to explain to you why I behaved as I did.'

'Oh, yes.' Her voice was bitter. 'You can rationalise your behaviour, Jay, but how can I rationalise mine? It was bad enough that I let you make love to me in the first place, but to feel about you the way I do now. Why? Why?' she cried out in despair. 'Why do I have to want you? There must be something wrong with me. I must be sick. The sort of woman who likes to be abused. Who wants . . .'

'No!' Now his voice was savage with suppressed pain and it silenced her. His hands cupped her face and looking at him Vicky could see her own pain mirrored in his eyes. 'Dear God, no, you mustn't think that about yourself.'

'Then what am I supposed to think, Jay?' she asked him tiredly. 'You know I want you, when you touch me, and not just physically but emotionally . . .' She was too exhausted to keep the truth from him any longer. 'I love you,' she told him with painful honesty, 'and it's tearing me apart.'

'Vicky, I think I have an explanation if you're prepared to listen to it.' He smiled faintly. 'I admit it's not very logical, but we're both human beings, not machines. Not everything can be explained by logic. I think that subconsciously we were attracted to one another right from the start. Maybe that attraction was too deep rooted for either of us to register it properly at the time, but it was there . . . I'd swear to it. Perhaps if I hadn't been so furiously angry about Jenny . . . so caught up in my anger, I might have recognised it. I don't know. Certainly I was aware of you, but then it was all swept away when I remembered Jenny and what she'd done to me. You were . . .'

'Just a female body to punish,' Vicky supplied for him.

'Yes, I'm afraid so ... You were all womankind and what I'd been made to suffer. I've never reacted to any other woman the way I have to you. From the moment we met again I wanted you—overwhelmingly so and not just in my bed but in my life. It was almost as though there was a subconscious recognition, and I think you felt it, too.'

She had, she acknowledged now. His words seemed to be soothing away her pain, making her see that whatever had motivated their actions had not really been important. If she had not been drunk and he had not been so savagely hurt and they had met at that party the history of their relationship would have been a different one, but she would still have been attracted to him, Vicky recognised.

'What happened in the past isn't something you should feel ashamed of Vicky. I know you suffered dreadfully for it, and I can't tell you what it does to me to know how much of the twins' life I have already missed ...'

'Last night, I thought perhaps it was them you wanted after all and not me,' she confessed huskily.

'I want it all,' he told her rawly. 'You ... the children we already have and those that hopefully we will have, but most of all I want your love.'

Deep inside Vicky felt herself tremble. What Jay had said to her made sense. She did love him, and perhaps he was right in suggesting that all those years ago they had subconsciously reached out to one another. The sickening sense of shame that had possessed her since she realised who he was had gone, burned away in the fires of passion. She felt cleansed, and empty of her previous guilt and self-loathing. It was as though she had undergone an emotional baptism and was finally free to leave the past.

'You have it.'

For a moment he looked at her and then his mouth touched hers, gently, lovingly, happiness flowered warmly inside her. She reached up to embrace him, aware of him in ways she had never been before, knowing that he was not invulnerable or indifferent. Whatever the explanation for what lay in the past, it was over now. They had the present and the future and suddenly she felt strong enough to reach out and embrace both.

She smiled at him and whispered, 'Let's go home ... I can't wait for us to start our life together. I love you so much, Jay.' Tears stung her eyes. 'I nearly threw it all away.'

'I wouldn't have let you,' he assured her. 'I was prepared to fight much harder for you than I had to, my love, and love is a mighty strong ally, too strong for us mere mortals to resist.'

Against his mouth she murmured his name and then forgot whatever it was she had been about to say in the slow sweet building of pleasure that filled her, and that she knew was filling him. Words could wait ... showing him her love could not.

# Harlequin Presents

## Coming Next Month

**903 MAN IN THE PARK Emma Darcy**
A receptionist, new to Sydney, makes friends with a man she meets in the park. But what gives him the right to insist that her boss—a dazzlingly attractive man—is all wrong for her?

**904 AN UNBREAKABLE BOND Robyn Donald**
A lawyer is furious when his late uncle's mistress inherits a large share in the family estate. But his contempt is overridden by passion whenever they are together.

**905 ONE IN A MILLION Sandra Field**
A lottery winner hightails it to a cottage in Cape Breton to reassess her worth. And when her neighbor sweeps her off her feet, she wonders, does he want her love—or her money?

**906 DIPLOMATIC AFFAIR Claire Harrison**
Ambition outweighed their love when he was a young diplomat in Washington and she was studying medicine. Seeing him again, she knows she won't survive another affair. But what if that's all he offers?

**907 DARK BETRAYAL Patricia Lake**
Even after three years away, an English fashion designer longs to give herself to a renowned playwright—body and soul—and forget she'd ever hoped for fidelity from him.

**908 PASSIONATE DECEPTION Mary Lyons**
After she creates a commotion at the company shareholders' annual meeting, a law student gets right in to see the chairman of Lancaster International. And he's positively furious—but more stimulated than he's felt in years.

**909 NO LONGER A DREAM Carole Mortimer**
After her fiancé's death, love seemed only a dream. But passion, at least, is possible when an author meets a film magnate, who challenges her to live life to the fullest again.

**910 A LASTING KIND OF LOVE Catherine Spencer**
They spent one glorious night together when she was an awkward girl. Now she's glad he doesn't recognize her. That way maybe their love will last forever.

Available in August wherever paperback books are sold, or through Harlequin Reader Service:

In the U.S.
P.O. Box 1397
Buffalo, N.Y.
14240-1397

In Canada
P.O. Box 2800, Postal Station A
5170 Yonge Street
Willowdale, Ontario M2N 6J3

# Harlequin "Super Celebration"
# SWEEPSTAKES

## NEW PRIZES—NEW PRIZE FEATURES & CHOICES—MONTHLY

**1.** To enter the sweepstakes, follow the instructions outlined on the Center Insert Card. Alternate means of entry, NO PURCHASE NECESSARY, you may also enter by mailing your name, address and birthday on a plain 3″ x 5″ piece of paper to: In U.S.A.: Harlequin "Super Celebration" Sweepstakes, P.O. Box 1867, Buffalo, N.Y. 14240-1867. In Canada: Harlequin "Super Celebration" Sweepstakes, P.O. Box 2800, 5170 Yonge Street, Postal Station A, Willowdale, Ontario M2N 6J3.

**2.** Winners will be selected in random drawings from all entries received. All prizes will be awarded. These prizes are in addition to any free gifts which might be offered. Versions of this sweepstakes with different prizes may appear in other presentations by TorStar and their affiliates. The maximum value of the prizes offered is $8,000.00. Winners selected will receive the prize offered from their prize package.

**3.** The selection of winners will be conducted under the supervision of Marden-Kane, an independent judging organization. By entering the sweepstakes, each entrant accepts and agrees to be bound by these rules and the decision of the judges which shall be final and binding. Odds of winning are dependent upon the total number of entries received. Taxes, if any, are the sole responsibility of the winners. Prizes are not transferable. This sweepstakes is scheduled to appear in Retail Outlets of Harlequin Books during the period of June 1986 to December 1986. All entries must be received by January 31st, 1987. The drawing will take place on or about March 1st, 1987 at the offices of Marden-Kane, Lake Success, New York. For Quebec (Canada) residents, any litigation regarding the running of this sweepstakes and the awarding of prizes must be submitted to La Regie de Lotteries et Course du Quebec.

**4.** This presentation offers the prizes as illustrated on the Center Insert Card.

**5.** This offer is open to residents of the U.S., and Canada, 18 years or older, except employees of TorStar, its affiliates, subsidiaries, Marden-Kane and all other agencies and persons connected with conducting this sweepstakes. All Federal, State and local laws apply. Void where prohibited or restricted by law. Winners will be notified by mail and may be required to execute an affidavit of eligibility and release which must be returned within 14 days after notification. Winners consent to the use of their name, photograph and/or likeness for advertising and publicity in conjunction with this and similar promotions without additional compensation. One prize per family or household. Canadian winners will be required to answer a skill testing question.

**6.** For a list of our most recent prize winners, send a stamped, self-addressed envelope to: WINNERS LIST, c/o Marden-Kane, P.O. Box 525, Sayreville, NJ 08872.

*No Lucky Number needed to win!*